STUMP

Born in Liverpool in 1966, Niall Griffiths now lives
in Wales. He has published three novels: *Grits*,
Sheepshagger and *Kelly + Victor*.

Niall Griffiths

STUMP

V

VINTAGE

Published by Vintage 2004

6 8 10 9 7

First published in Great Britain in 2003 by
Jonathan Cape

Vintage
Random House, 20 Vauxhall Bridge Road,
London SW1V 2SA

www.vintage-books.co.uk

Addresses for companies within
The Random House Group Limited can be found at:
www.randomhouse.co.uk/offices.htm

The Random House Group Limited Reg. No. 954009

A CIP catalogue record for this book
is available from the British Library

ISBN 9780099287582

The Random House Group Limited supports the Forest Stewardship
Council (FSC®), the leading international forest certification organisation.
Our books carrying the FSC label are printed on FSC® certified paper. FSC
is the only forest certification scheme endorsed by the leading environmental
organisations, including Greenpeace. Our paper procurement policy can be
found at www.randomhouse.co.uk/environment

Printed and bound by CPI Group (UK) Ltd, Croydon, CR0 4YY

Acknowledgements

A section of this novel, in somewhat different form, appeared in the *New Welsh Review*, Number 57. My thanks to the editor, Francesca Rhydderch.

Big thanks, in no particular order, to: Neville Gomes; Gray Bass, Emma and Ben; Pete Jenks; Stephen Hanna; Brian D.; Spud Prowse; Gid Cleary, Della, and their baby; and Josh Tyree – a singular voice of reason from across the Atlantic. And to the Cardiff collective: Des and Helen, John and Charlotte, Lloyd and Sal, Bridget Keehan, Claire Wallace.

I'm also indebted to several sources of information: for the cell/brain stuff, John Ratey's *A User's Guide to the Brain* (Little, Brown, 2001); for the information on the properties of light, Joel Aschenbach's essay 'The Power of Light' in the *National Georgraphic*, October 2001; for the bird descriptions, several field guides to the birdlife of Northern Europe, among them Larousse's; sources too numerous to list (on paper, celluloid and in the real world) for the NA/AA material; and for the 'cognitive dissonance' stuff I'd like to thank the superb work on www.anxietyculture.com along with every pointless mind-murdering job I've ever done under every egomaniacal fuckwit of a boss and every teacher pale with loathing for themselves and for us because we weren't more like them.

Live long, all of youse.

To the Meachen family:

Clive
Maureen
Tom
Sean
Emily

For them the bitings of grasshoppers and flies killed, neither was there found any remedy for their life: for they were worthy to be punished by such.

But thy sons not the very teeth of venomous dragons overcame: for thy mercy was over by them, and healed them.

For they were pricked, that they should remember thy words.

Wisdom of Solomon, 16:9–11, Apocrypha

'. . . it was related that the party of explorers, at the extremity of their strength, had the constant delusion that there was *one more member* than could actually be counted.'

T. S. Eliot, referring to
Shackleton's Antarctic expedition

KITCHEN

He came down into me garden again this mornin, the fox, thee ahl fox with the one eye. Round about dawn, I mean the sky was still more night than day like, still a moon up there there was, an he came down off the mountain an through the hedge an into me garden, sniffed around the rabbit hutch for a bit then ate the cold bits of chip an fish batter I'd left out for him last night. Wolfed them as if he was starving, as if he hadn't eaten in weeks, then cocked his leg an pissed on me cabbages an fucked off back through the hedge an back up again on to the mountain.

I stood at the kitchen sink, staring out through the window, watchin him. He didn't notice me, or if he did, he wasn't arsed; it didn't bother him, my shape at the window. Me rabbit, Charlie, was safe asleep in me bedroom, in a box lined with an ahl jumper under-neath the bed, an me pulse raced an me skin crawled from the vile nightmare that'd woken me up so I came into the kitchen for some water an a fag an saw the tawny shape low in the mornin mist through the greasy glass. Them highsteppin paws, so delicate the way he lifts them an puts them down. Thin winter ribs under the russet fur an the white-tipped tail arched high over his back an his pointed muzzle probing through the dewy mist like the prow a ship. An the one green eye glinting an then the fox-shaped hole in the mist as he turned an went away again so sudden, back through the hedge an up on to Pen Dinas, the head of the town, where I suppose he lives.

This wild animal in me garden. This talented predator, here in my head.

I gulped water an watched the mist tendril in to refill the hole made by his absence. Me skin dried, me heartbeat slowed back to normal. Me stump stopped itching or, rather, the void at the end of it did. The hole. Thee emptiness. The sick an warty shapes of me nightmare just dissolved like salt in water an I could feel me sanity, me hard-won fuckin sanity, me sanity gained at the cost of a fuckin *limb*, bein painlessly restored. That wild fox in me garden. Little red one-eyed wolf come down off the mountain into my living space to eat the scraps I'd left out for him an pee on me strugglin cabbages. Bein visited by that wild thing.

How I fucking love this.

Drank me water, smoked me fag, went back to me still-warm bed. Checked on Charlie, wee white fluffy slumberin bundle in the shadows beneath me mattress an I climbed on to that mattress an slept for another three hours. Nightmareless, whimperless sleep. Unusual an needed. Would've slept longer but Charlie woke me up by sniffin at me face. Little big-eared lettuce-breathin hoppin bastard.

Fox.

Try an make yer breakfast with one fuckin arm; take the kettle over to the sink, put it down on the drainin board, turn the cold tap on, pick the kettle up again an fill it, put it down again, turn the tap off, pick the kettle up again, put it down again an work thee attachment into the socket an flick it on. Open the cupboard door, take the mug out an put it down on the worktop, close the cupboard door, take a tea bag out of the box an put it in the mug. Open the fridge door, take milk out, put milk down on the floor while you unscrew the top, pour a drop into the mug then put the bottle back on the floor again while you put the top back on then replace it in the fridge an close the door. Open another cupboard door, remove a bowl an put it on the worktop, close the cupboard door. Take the box of Ricicles an hold it between what's left of yer left arm an yer ribs on that side while you unfurl the plastic inner wrapper with yer good hand, your *only* hand, tip the box an shake some cereal into the bowl, put it between yer stump an ribs again an rescrew up the inner wrapper with yer one hand an put the box back an then say 'shite' cos you've forgotten to leave the milk out, after nearly two fuckin long one-armed years you've still forgotten to leave the friggin milk out. So it's *back* to the fridge, open it, milk out, floor, unscrew, stand, pour, bend, rescrew, replace in fridge, close door again. Take a spoon out of the cutlery drawer, close cutlery drawer. Back to kettle which has clicked off now, pour boiling water into mug, put spoon into bowl of popping cereal an take it into the front room, put it down on coffee table, turn telly on. Return to kitchen, agitate the tea bag in the mug with a spoon until the liquid turns brownish, then delve in the box of sugar cubes which you buy instead of loose sugar because cubes are easier to deal with one-handedly an take up two cubes an drop them in the mug. Scoop wilted bag out with spoon, drop it in bin, put spoon in sink then take up tea an go back into the front room, where news on the telly informs you of more countrywide train disruptions, delays an cancellations, not that yer plannin on travellin anywhere. Blow on to cool an then sip tea. When you eat the cereal, leave the bowl on the coffee table an lean over it an scoop it up into yer mouth. Put the spoon in the bowl whenever you need a sip of tea cos you've got no other hand to hold the mug with.

Ridiculous empty sleeve floppin an a-flappin down yer body. Nowt fuckin in it, no, just a daft an empty fuckin sleeve.

So try an make yer breakfast with one fuckin arm. It'll be a frustrating, exasperating pain in the fuckin arse but you'll do it. Now try washin up the breakfast dishes with that same one arm. Now try rolling a fuckin cigarette. Try gettin dressed, or undressed. Try gardening; try turnin the soil, sowin the seeds, harvestin yer fuckin vegetables. Try, fuck, makin a lasagne for yer tea; the pure *mess* it makes. Which you've got to clear up; an with just one hand, as well. You'll manage to do all these things, they'll all get done. Take twice as friggin long, like, an you'll end up bootin dents in yer walls, but you'll *do* them. Not easy, but you'll get them done. Only easy thing to do with one hand is have a thrap, providin yeh do it without any pictorial assistance. Unless yeh lie on yer back with a box of tissues on yer chest an yer *Razzle* propped precariously up against that box, except then you have to interrupt the thrap every time yeh need to turn a page

4

an sometimes the magazine slides down an off an then you have to rearrange the whole set-up an yer old feller goes limp an you end up throwin everythin to the floor an shouting. All yeh wanted was a quick wank for the relief in it, like, an now look – the pure fuckin *frustration*. It's rubbish.

I smoke two Lamberts with me tea then take the dishes into the kitchen an dump em in the sink. Wash em later. With the tepid dregs of the tea I neck two codeine then go into the bathroom an turn the shower on. Try brushin yer teeth with one arm; try just puttin toothpaste on the brush. Scouring an scrubbin all the bad night-mucus from yer gob an then suddenly you realise you've just been standin here for some time, holdin the brush still against yer front teeth, just staring down into the featureless porcelain of the sink. Must a been stood like this for five minutes or more; the bathroom's filled up with steam an there's drool an froth on me chin as if I'm rabid. Thinkin about nothing, standin here like a statue for all that time just starin down, absolutely fuck all in me head. Where do I go to when I'm like that? Do I stay here? Or what else comes into me? All me memories n hopes n stuff, all the shite that makes me me, where does it all go when I go off on one into them trances?

Don't know. Don't know *what* fuckin happens. All I know is that I feel perfectly at peace.

There's a whole day ahead. So many things can happen in this one day. Me stomach lurches at the thought of it. As it always has, for as long as I can remember. Lurched, recoiled away from life an the days we have to spend.

Step into the shower, ow, yeh bastard, too hot. I turn the cold tap an wait for the spray to cool. Me left arm, the truncated arm on me left side; the doctor says it's healed incredibly well but I can't stop seeing in it evidence of infection – a red discoloration, some sensation of heat. Sometimes even a smell, a bad whiff like milk gone sour. Seems okay today, tho. I can even admire the way the skin has been so smoothly stitched and has so seamlessly grown back into itself. It's as if I was born this way; as if I've only ever been one-armed. Or one-and-a-*half*-armed. This little thing jerking at me left shoulder, I've never been any different, never looked any different; I've always had a limb made up of one part flesh, one part air. Thee entire atmosphere for a left forearm, that's what I've always had.

Our capacity to regenerate. The ways we can rebuild arselves, as Peter fuckin Salt might've said with one of his benign an pitying smiles on that grizzled fuckin face.

Right, fuckin *move*, man, get the day done; get clean an dried an dressed. Put the new fleece on, the nice new Blackwatch tartan fleece, an pin thee arm up an gather together life's, movement's, paraphernalia; ciggies an lighter an wallet an keys, all that stuff. Pick the rabbit up out of his poo corner (clean up them little pellets later) an go out into the garden an put him back in his hutch, rip a radish up out of the soil an stick that in there with him. Tickle his head, tell him you'll be back soon. Sniff, deeply, the fox's left scent, the memory of him; his hot an thick, blade-sharp musk. Think how ace the day will be; one of

6

them clear an crisp spring days, cold but the sun shining, light so honed it will make every leaf, every blade of grass adopt a purely individual shade of green. It will turn the sea into a million mirrors. It will make the stump ache an throb, give me a fuckin migraine in thee elbow. But still.

Back through the flat, telly off, front window open a tad for the fresh air. Charlie's wee mings. Leave the house by the front door, turn left an start walking, down towards the harbour an the dump, past the Welsh-language primary school where the frost overnight has made grey flowers on the railings. No it hasn't; what it's done is stick itself to thee invisible flowers that bloom perennially on the metal. It's stuck to them, given them form.

Here comes another day. Another day I'm alive in. Me an me rabbit an me one-eyed fox.

Step 1: We admitted that we were powerless over our addictions, that our lives had become unmanageable. And that we would willingly surrender up any last shred of self-autonomy we felt we may have possessed to a judgemental and sanctimonious gobshite in a small smoky yellow room in St Helens and the vast and frightening organisation behind him. And we admitted not only that we were completely worthless but also that if we should ever renege on this cession then we would become even less; not just shit, but the parasites on that shit. The parasites on the shit of the parasites on that shit. But here's ar white flag, all the fuckin same. Look at us, we're waving it. With just one fucking arm.

7

CAR

They depart the city at Speke, where, at a roundabout, the A562 becomes the A561 and signs give directions to AIRPORT and SPEKE HALL and RUNCORN and NORTH WALES/QUEENSFERRY. On their left is a wide escarpment of council houses, uniformly redbrick, over which a jet soars on a slant, leaving the earth in a heat-shimmer trousseau with the nearing sun bouncing off airborne glass and steel. To their right somewhere, beyond the derelict factory complex now brownly crumbling, is the estuary and beyond that their goal. They are driving a Morris Minor, jalopy dilapidated, which trembles and coughs and threatens to disintegrate whenever Darren Taylor, the driver, attempts to gun the engine. To pick up some speed. To more quickly get where they are going.

—Fuckin useless mudderfucker *cunt* of a car . . . fuckin Tommy givin us *this* pure piecer fuckin wank . . .

Alastair the passenger does not look up from the *Reader's Digest Book of the Road* he is studying balanced on his trackie'd knees.

—Yeh want Runcorn.

—I know I want Runcorn, Ally. I *know* me way out of the fuckin city.

—Runcorn, an then we can gerron to the M56 til . . . Hapsford or somewhere, wharrever the fuck it's

8

called. Junction 14. Then straight through ter Chester
an from there onter thee A55 down towards Bala.

—CUNT!

Darren gives the wanker sign through the window
to a Bedford van too close to his wing. The driver of
that van looks down into the Morris, sees them there
– Darren's fingers thick with sovereign rings, his tight
short curly hair, square jaw set below his bulging black-
scooped eyes, and his baseball-capped passenger, face
stoat-sharp leering weak chin hidden in the shiny
collar of his tracksuit – and drops back, away.

Darren's face relaxes. —Fuckin prick.

—Useter go fishin at Bala with me grandad when
I was a kid, like. Caught a fuckin pike once. *Yowge*
fuckin thing it was, teeth like six-inch nails. No messin.

They turn off towards Runcorn. As they leave the
roundabout and enter the dual carriageway Darren puts
his foot down and the old engine bellows like a bull.

—Jesus fuckin Christ, this heaper fuckin *shite*.
Gunner av werds with that twat Tommy when we get
back, shit you not, Ally. Be surprised if we even *get* to
fuckin Wales in this piler fuckin shit. Takin the piss,
that cunt. Yeh don't send two of yer best boys off on
a straightener in a fuckin shed like this, lar, tellin yeh.
Takin. The fuckin. *Piss*.

Alastair closes the road book and slides it off his
knees. —Yeh. Should've lent us the Shogun.

—The Shogun? Fucks. Mudderfucker loves that
fuckin thing moren he loves is own fuckin kids. Not
that I blame im on *that* one, like; seen is kids? Ugly
little fuckers, tellin yeh. Take them wheels over them
snot-nosed sprogs any fuckin day. Too right.

9

—The Vitara, then.

—Well, yeh, that's what *I* said, the Vitara. But oh no; that cunt Jamie's off up to fuckin Scotland in it, inny? Meetin some boys in Glasgow. Needs to maken impression, see.

—Jamie?

—Yeh.

—Which one?

—Squires. Him with the gozzy eye.

Alastair knows Gozzy-eye Jamie, wonders what it'd be like to perceive the world through a squint. He crosses his eyes and succeeds only in blurring the dashboard and the passing world, flat featureless fields and houses, outside the car.

Lights flash on the road. Another Morris Minor approaching them in the opposite direction; the driver flashes his lights once and smiles and waves as he passes.

—Look, there's another one. Second time this mornin. What's their fuckin problem? Why do thee keep on fuckin flashin us?

—Same car, innit, Alastair says.

—So fuckin what, like?

—It's just summin thee do. Thee just crack on to each other, like, in these ahl cars.

Darren sneers. —Dozy arseholes.

But it's like animals, is the thought or something like it going through Alastair, exotic animals or something. Like some instinctive recognition of some shared thing in a stranger that offers the approximation of a companionship and the possible protection harboured therein. Like: See this, look, I'm not alone in the world. Like some insistence on and projection of the self, a distress flare fired in the hope of an answer and such a response comes and you swell and it is too vague for explication but welcomed.

Darren yawns. —Fuckin shattered, me, Ally. Good night last night, wannit?

—You know it.

—Could do with a bumper that gack of Peter's, fuckin wake me up, like. Be asleep before fuckin Wales.

—Djer bring any with yis?

—Bugle? Nah. Ad be fuckin snortin it if I ad've done, woulden I?

—Why didn't yeh bring any, well?

—Cos we *can't* fuck this up, lar. Imagine it; some sheepshagger bizzy pulls us over for speedin or jumpin a red or wharrever, sees ar eyes, like, searches the motor. We'd be pure fucked. Imagine what Tommy'd do. Ar lives woulden be werth friggin livin, lar.

—Yeh. Is right.

—So I left all temptations back home. Just avter purrup with it, won't we? This well-borin fuckin drive. Not even a tape player or anythin. Can't even av any tunes.

—Least we're gettin paid tho.

—Yeh, fifty fuckin notes. Hundred if we find him, which I doubt very much we fuckin will. Shite. Could earn fifty notes on the fuckin dip down Ally Dock in a couple of fuckin hours.

Runcorn suburb, a row of shops; newsagent's, bookies, laundry, Sayer's the Bakers, chipper and Chinese. Another newsagent's on the end. Darren stops at a zebra crossing at which a young woman waits. He smiles at her as she crosses in front of the car and she smiles back a bit nervously and looks away as his gaze follows her, his eyes locked laser-like to her arse. Growly voice:

—G'wahn, love. Over yeh go. An can I blosh on yer fuckin chin, by the way?

Alastair laughs. A middle-aged man in a paint-streaked blue boiler suit carrying a Sayer's bag makes to follow the girl but Darren revs and slams into gear and the car leaps out in front of the man missing him by mere inches. He shouts and leaps back on to the pavement and stumbles over the kerb and drops his bag and sausage rolls spill out and break.

—Not *you*, yeh fat ahl twat! Youse can fuckin wait!

Darren cackles, as does Alastair. They pass a hitch-hiker holding up a sign saying 'HEREFORD' and Darren beeps at him and they both give him the wanker sign and leave him behind. There is some more laughter.

—Knob'ed. Get the fuckin bus, lad.

—Yeh.

—Where the fuck *is* bleedin Hereford, anyway, Ally?

—Dunno. Alastair shrugs. —We're headin for Chester.

—Yeh, an where to after that?

—Bala.

—Nah, I mean, where are we *going* to? What's ar, like, destination?

—Aberystwyth.

Darren smiles and shakes his head. —Makes me laugh, the way yeh say that werd. Sounds like yer fuckin garglin or summin. Don't know how yis can say em anyway, all these mad fuckin names.

—Llandderfel. *Rhiw*las.

—Shurrup, will yeh. Yer coverin me in fuckin yocker. Yeh know Bala Lake, like? That's not water, yeh know. It's fuller fuckin spit from all the locals tryin to say where thee live.

—What, Bala? That's easy.

—No, yeh know. Thee other places *around* it, like.

They make a right turn at a roundabout, following a sign for FRODSHAM. Down a slip road on to the motorway, smoothly out into the steady stream of traffic southbound into Wales. The car's engine and Alastair's belly rumble and mutter together.

—That your fuckin belly, lad?

—Yeh. Fuck me, am starvin.

—Are yeh?

—Yeh. Pure fuckin Hank.

—We'll stop at a place just over the border well an get summin to eat. There's a postie a wanner check out anyway, see if it's screwable.

—Can't wait that long. I could eat a scabby head.

—Well, yill fuckin well have to fuckin wait cos we're not fuckin stoppin til we're over the fuckin border. Should've made some friggin butties or somethin, shouldn't yeh?

—I did. Marmite ones, but I left em in the fuckin kitchen.

—Marmite? Eeee God. Pure fuckin *hangin* that shit, lar. Even if yeh hadder brought em yeh woulden be fuckin eatin the fuckers cos as soon as yeh took em out the bag thee'd be *straight* out that friggin winda. Can't even stand the fuckin *smell* of that stuff, me. Makes me fuckin heave. Smell that?

—What?

—Sniff up. *That's* what fuckin Marmite smells like.

The smell creeping into the car is the sulphurous stink from the Shotton steelworks rising above the flat wide bog on their left, chimneys and towers charred and blackened between marsh and mudflat like some odd settlement, some city, oneiric and liminal, peopled by shapes of flame and smoulder which exude the blooms of oily smoke departing the scorched towers for the contused sky above. Slim and close-stacked citadels whose purpose is to percolate from the mud of mire and estuary some semblance of those who through rot and dissolution assiduous and saline made such mud, this shit, re-distil into traceable shape what flesh as has liquefied and glooped into what choking approximation or facsimile asthmatic as these upward-drifting reaching great wraiths of greasy steam. These sky-bent and cloud-prone precipitates seen only nocturnally in their honest form – tremendous balls of flame.

—Ey, Alastair.

No response; Alastair is gazing out at the distant steelworks. His nose is pressed up against the window, his cap pushed back on his head by the peak against the glass. Small, comma-shaped seborrhoeic stain made by the touching tip of his nose.

Darren elbows him not gently in the ribs.

—Ow! What the fuck was that for?

—I'm fuckin asking yis a question.

—What?

—What does a bloke who's shagged loads of women have for breakfast?

—Dunno.

—Yeh, Darren sneers. —I thought as much.

—Oh fuck off.

Darren laughs. Frodsham and Shotton disappear behind them and then so too does the small stretch of motorway and they are on an A-road once more. This one will provide them passage into Chester.

LANDFILL

Sunlight in shards. Bright spikes of light. Light from
the sun hits the sea and shatters and becomes sealight,
wavelight, waterlight. Exists as a wave outside in the
world but becomes a particle inside me head, through
me eyes, and, fuck, imagine if I had've lost an eye
instead of an arm; no more the dual spear of the sun.
No more the squint an blink when it darts at you
from water or glass or chrome.

Such light as this in me dreams. Always this briefly
blindin light in me dreams. Feel saturated by this light
I do, this white light off the sea; become part of me
it has – like, in photon nuclei, the electron orbits so
far away. A nucleus the size of a five-pence coin, the
electron would be two miles away. Beings of light and
space we are, this bright light in me eyes, this space
here in me sleeve, an both them things in me head.

I turn up off the harbour road on to Pen-yr-Angor.
The stink from the landfill hits me, a thick, cheesy
reek. I sit on a bench by thee old World War II pillbox
to smoke a ciggie before heading onwards, down into
that smell.

You can feel a kind of kinship here, with and in
this light. A closeness, like. It's always here, skimming
off the sea, it can give yeh a root, some sort of definition. A hundred and twenty-five million rods an

cones in ar eyes, a fifth of yer brain does nowt but try to deal with the visual world, the retina bein an extension of the brain, rods respondin to dim light unable to detect colour an cones the sensors of colour wavelengths, the spectrum like, capturin things both wave an particle that travels at 186,282 miles per second an the vast distances it covers to reach us, the incredible space it brings to us. I mean, can yeh smell or hear Jupiter's moons? The Milky Way? What sound does the sun make as it burns, an does it smell of ash?

But the ways there are to capture light; a snake's thin slit, a fly's bulgin black honeycomb, ar own strange bulbous jellies. Light between us an everythin else, you must look through light at the world; like them mountains down the coast there, thee appear bluish to me cos there's sky between me an them. There's airlight. I'm lookin at them mountains through a mass of blue sky.

It'll be alright. Evrythin's gunner be okay.

I flick the stub into the harbour. A few seagulls descend squabbling on it then when thee realise it's inedible thee fuck complaining off. Their funny little danglin feet, like slices of boiled ham. That Scouse lad Colm told me once that he found a dead body in this harbour, a dead woman like. The way he described her; all bloated an soft, 'like feta fuckin cheese', those were his words. Bet the gulls had a friggin feast. Bet thee pure friggin loved it. Colm seemed to love it n all, to tell the truth; likes to embrace the dark things, Colm does. Seems to actively *enjoy* the desperation in life. Haven't seen im for a while; true, I've been avoidin him, yeh, I mean he's too much of a fuckin leader into temptation that boy an I didn't know im that well to begin with, but you'd think we'd bump into each other around town evry now an again, wouldn't yeh? Maybe he's buggered off, like his girlfriend did. The mad alky one – Mairead. She did one a year or two ago apparently. Everybody seems to, after a while.

Back on to the dump road, into the thickening stink. Bright sun today but it's cold; winter's still hangin on, an there are big dark clouds to the north, over Cader Idris. Me stump starts to throb in me sleeve but there's fuck all I can do about that except try n ignore it, so I focus on the top of Pen Dinas, the monument all the way up there, itself built by a one-armed feller, a veteran of the Napoleonic Wars. He carted all the stones an mortar all that way himself – well, him an a few donkeys, like. But still some fuckin feat, that; buildin the scaffolding, mixin the compo, laying them big stones, all with just the one arm. Fuckin amazin, really. Amazin what yeh can do, how yer'll survive. Isn't that right, Mr Salt? Yeh, you *know* it is.

There's a buzzard soarin around the monument. Wings spread, eyes locked on to the ground, lookin for rats on the dump or rabbits on the hillsides. Thee see piss, buzzards do, all birds of prey; that's how thee find their food, thee see thee ultraviolet glow of its piss. *We* can't, like, cos anythin below four hundred nanometres is invisible to ar eyes; ultraviolet, X-ray, gamma rays. A world within this one that we'll never, ever perceive.

So many hours in libraries I've spent. Anythin to beat the boredom.

I see the buzzard swoop. Bank and tuck an plummet.

Some little furry feller has come to some torn an spurting end. Small bones breaking. Hope Charlie's okay; but he will be, I'm sure, I gave him a radish before I left an put him in his hutch. He'll be grand. He'll just sleep an nibble an twitch the day away. Wonder if he misses things, if he pines in some buried species memory for cool dark tunnels in thee earth or hillsides in the sunshine or sprinting across a meadow. Wonder if he misses the company of other bunnies. I remember, as a kid, bein taken to North Wales somewhere, probly Talacre or somewhere, by me mam during one of the myxomatosis outbreaks; the rabbits stumblin around the campsite, bloody froth in their ears, eyes like pus-filled eggcups . . . I can still remember watchin one scratch its own eye out. Scratch with the big back leg an pop, there was thee eye, danglin, leakin . . . I was about seven years old. Robbed me of sleep for weeks, that did.

But Charlie'll be okay. He's my responsibility, Charlie is.

A wave breaks in foamlight, straight into me eye. It starts to water. Should've brought some sunglasses.

It'll be alright. Don't you worry, it's all gunner be fine.

I turn a corner. The gates to the dump, open, an just beyond them is Peredur's shack; wooden an ramshackle with a corrugated-iron roof pitched black, it gets like a fuckin oven in there in summertime an I don't know how Perry can stand it, but he's always in there, in that flea-bitten mangy ahl donkey jacket he wears. I don't think he's able to take it off any more; I think it's, like, *grown* into his skin. He's wearin it now as he answers the door; that, an some ahl suit, kex shiny with muck, an great big army boots with the soles flappin off.

—Iya, Perry.

—Shwmae, mate. In yew come then.

There's yellow stubble on his face and his hair's all lank an knotted. But the whites of his eyes are just that, white an not yellow an there's no booze-stink on his breath. He catches me assessing look an shakes his head.

—Don't be worryin. Still dry I am, still clean. Still fuckin sober an bored to fuckin death. Yew?

I close the door behind me. Pupils expand instantly, searchin the gloom for some light. —Exactly the friggin same, my man. Dry as a bone an climbin the fuckin walls.

He looks at me worried as he sits in his armchair. I shake me head an take a seat opposite him. —Nah, don't worry. Nowt to worry about. I'm grand, I'm alright.

—Been to-a meetings then?

—Nah, not for a few months, no. Why would I wanner sit in a poky room drinkin crap coffee an listenin to a loader deadheads whinge on? Fuck that. I'm managin fine on me own.

And I am.

—One day at a time, boy, innit?

—That's what thee say, aye. What's that yer readin?

I nod at the big thick coverless hardback on Perry's side table. He holds it up; a copy, ancient by the looks of it, of the King James Bible complete with Apocrypha.

—The Bible? Thought yer'd read that loadser times,

mate. I mean yer always bleedin quotin from the fuckin thing.

—Oh I yav, aye, but this is-a apocryphal books, see. All-a stuff that-a Church elders at the time, the fuckin Fat Controllers like, wanted-a leave out, didn't want yew to see. Makes yew think, it does. Ever read it yewerself then?

—What, the Bible? Nah. Started to, once, like, but couldn't really get on with it. Found the main character clumsily drawn; too obviously a Christ figure.

Perry laughs. —Want some tea?

I don't really, but I nod yeh. It's just thee act of raising a cup or glass to me lips an swallowin liquid; just that simple act. Helps, in however tiny a way, to suppress the cravings.

—Wharrabout yerself, Perry?

—What about me what?

—The meetings, like. Been to any yerself recently?

He places a blackened kettle on a camping stove. Takes two tin mugs down from a shelf.

—Last week.

—Yer didn't lapse, did yis?

—No. But I sure as all fuck would've if I hadna gone.

Me heart feels a wee bit heavier for a moment. Perry's bent back, so thin inside that heavy coat, the top of his tatty head so vulnerable n soft, so easily crushed.

—What brought it on, lad?

A shrug of those small shoulders. —Can't say, really. Fuck, mun, yew know how it goes. Fuckin boredom. Fuckin deadness evrywhere. Yewer central fuckin nervous system all over-a bastard place, *yew* know how it goes.

—That's what the librium's for, tho, innit? Didn't yer take any?

—Thirty bastard mil, aye.

—An it didn't work?

A blue flame bursts underneath the kettle, lapping round its charred base. Peredur stands an shuffles like an old man over to his seat an sits down again. Brushes imaginary dust off his knees.

—*Nothing* fuckin works sometimes, boy. Yew know that.

An he's right, I do. Know it only too fuckin well. Wet an spectacular wreckage leads to 'powerful forgetting' which leads to 'periodics' which lead to the 'dry drunks' which go to 'immersion' an 'enabler' an 'therapeutic alliance' an any alternative, any fuckin alternative atropine aversion therapy or Antabuse or ECT or acufuckinpuncture or snakepits or swimmin with dolphins an all of that all of it comes completely back to this one pure an irreducible phenomenon: a booming heart that burns to drink.

—Well . . . least yis didn't lapse. Didn't drink, like. Shoulda given me a knock.

Pathetic, but I can't think of anythin else to say. Perry rolls a ciggie.

—Aye. But, well, I'm sittin yur, yew know how it is, sittin in that room like, a shakes, a sobs, a sweats, drinkin eyr coffee by-a bastard gallon, chain-smokin, an it's all that daft fuckin holdin hands an shoutin 'yewer worth it' at each other, an all iss fuckin shite, like . . .

22

I nod. Remember that shit only *too* fuckin well.

—Yeh.

—An in comes iss young lad, only about eighteen like, he've had a slip, like, or maybe it was his first time yur an he comes fallin through-a door, spew down is shirt like, cachar in his trousers, I mean he was in *some* bad fuckin state. Eyes all over-a place, what looks like white cornflakes all round his lips an chin . . .

Nod again. The things that booze can do to yer skin. The scaly, leaking things.

—An he stands yur, like, swayin, goes to speak an spews blood . . .

A bigger nod. Oesophageal varices; varicose veins in the throat from the poisons in booze and the strain of vomiting. Alcohol causes these to expand an eventually burst, causing blood puke.

—An I'm watchin im, like, iss mess of a boy standin yur weepin in a pool a piss an blood, an d'yew know what I thought? D'yew know-a first fuckin thought that came into my fuckin head?

—I think I can guess.

—'Yew lucky, fucking, *bastard.' That's* what I thought about that wreck of a yewman being. Wish *I* was as drunk as yew. Jesus Christ.

He shakes his head. There seems a vast sadness in him but then it's gone instantly as the kettle begins to whistle an he hands me the rolled cigarette an smiles an says:

—But anyway. I didn't drink, I got through it, an yer I fuckin am. Still clean an sober still. Strong as a fuckin ox.

—Fair play to yis.

—Oh aye. Chwarae teg, innit? Get through fuckin anythin, me, boy. Get through fuckin anything.

He pats me on the shoulder as he passes, turns the flame off an makes the tea. That boy at the meeting, the one Perry's just described, he's threatenin to come flailin into me head an make himself comfortable so I light the roll-up an look around the shack, marvellin at how Perry's furnished the whole place from items scavenged from the dump, from the telly an video in the corner on the packin crate to the stack of hard Europorn he thinks I don't know about beneath the camp bed against the back wall. He's been dump custodian for ages, Perry has; he says he's the only person he knows who's built his life for free. He's also very nearly destroyed it several times, at great expense, but then so have a million others. Including meself. An it's helped him to keep off the substances as well, I reckon; he loves it, he says, exploring the dump, what people discard. Says it's his own trove of treasure.

Christ, the boredom. The things we'll do to defeat it. The things we do to fill ar days, ar long, long days of drudgery and dreariness an living fuckin death, ar time on this planet the flat blank pattern of ar days.

—Yer yew go then.

He hands me a mug of tea.

—Ta.

He sits back down again. Smiling now; it's all gone, that desperation of a minute or two ago, frigged off from him. The mood swings of the dry alky. Startling extremes of the chronic dipso who just happens to be not drinking at the mo.

—How's-a arm?

—Half cremated.

I blow on an sip me tea.

—I was thinking.

—Oh, Christ, no.

—No, listen, wouldn't it've been better if yew hadder lost yewer *right* arm instead-a yewer left?

—Why?

—Cos yewer right-handed, aren't yew? So every time yew had a wank yew'd have to use yewer left an it'd feel like someone else doin it.

He laughs. I do as well, even tho I've heard that joke ten thousand fuckin times. *Made* that fuckin same joke on a fair few occasions as well.

—No but. It's fine tho, yeh?

—What?

—The bloody *arm*, boy. No pain or anythin?

—No, it's grand. Bit itchy sometimes, like, but that's all.

—Itchy?

—Yeh. I don't mean the arm itself, like, the, yer know, stump. I mean, yer know – the space.

—Ah. A phantom limb thing.

—Yeh.

—Peculiar carry-on that, innit.

—It is, yeh. Doctor explained it to me once.

—Oh aye? An what did he say?

I tell Perry what I remember, an what I've read, an what I on some new level that's appeared only since I became an amputee know; that thee ongoing business of this world, its fuss and clamour, imprints itself on ar neural networks at a very early age, an that these networks, so wide in their mesh an so sensitive, remain

25

in a state primed to experience certain sensations which they rapidly become accustomed to. These networks remain in a state of readiness to receive input even when a limb has gone, so they, an not the missing limb, continue to experience sensation. The downside to this is that abnormal pain an prickly sensations can become more pronounced with the passage of time, because the fake-pain network fires more an more, seeking to communicate with a receptor which has vanished, thus becoming more responsive to a random stimulus such as pain. An that always comes through, doesn't it, that particular random stimulus. Regard the stochastic resonance an wait for a shape to take; you *know* what that shape will be. Anywhere between these two responses: 'Ow, gerroff' and 'Make it stop please make it stop please God make this stop.'

—Knowmean? Understand?

—I do, aye, Perry nods. —What gets me tho yur is . . . I mean, this is an example of yewer brain bein unable to change. But it *does* change, tho, dunnit? I mean, yew can change it yewerself.

—Suppose.

—I mean in a sense of fillin in gaps. It's like-a booze; that goes, an it leaves one great big bastard hole. So yew fill it, don't yew.

—With what?

Perry waves his arm, indicating the shack walls an the bizarre sculptures he's decorated them with; fantastic shapes made from dump junk, pipes an planks an flattened tin cans. Strange hybrids, manifestations of the drink-warped contours of Peredur's mind which, as if to illustrate its twisting an prove the notion that thee abiding addiction is not to drugs or drink but to chaos itself, immediately jumps to focus on another subject: that of recent visitors to the dump, both animal an human. Of which there's lots, pickin through the ruins.

—Even adder bloody badger last week I did, down yur. Watched him for ages through me binox. Snufflin round for ages he was, God knows what he was lookin for. Red kites as well, tho eyr always around, on-a lookout for a seagull, see, too old or sick to flap away. An a fox n all, bold bugger he is, comes right up to outside-a shack if I leave scraps out for him. Only got one eye, he has.

One-eyed fox; *my* one-eyed fox? I won't tell Perry that he visits me too; I'm gunner keep him a secret. My one-eyed fox comin down off the mountain into me garden. I'll tell no one about him. He's me secret.

—An a hospital wagon called down-a other day. Dumpin a load-a stuff off. Nowt organic, like, no, ey incinerate all that stuff. Dangerous it is, see.

Organic stuff – like dressings. Like limbs. Lopped-off limbs bein chucked into the flames.

—But I got a nice present for yew, tho. Perry grins.
—A nice surprise. Should av it ready this evening.
—A prezzie?
—Oh aye.
—What is it?
—Not tellin yew, mun. It's a surprise. Might drop it round this evening.
—That'd be nice. Could do with a surprise.
—Couldn't we all, mun. But *yew've* got one, tho. From me.

—Ace.

I finish me tea an stand up. —Talkin of hospitals . . .

—Yew've got-a go up yur, av yew?

The worry on his face. Strange man, Peredur.

—Not thee ozzy, no. The doctor's. Just a check-up an that, y'know.

We say ar taras an I leave the shack an out through the gates, passin Perry's first delivery of the day; a truck overflowin with compressed cardboard boxes. The light has dimmed a bit an it seems like the clouds I noticed earlier to the north are creepin down this way, but there's still a lot of activity down the Pen-yr-Angor lane, a lot of bird activity; finches flittin in an out of the hedgerows, starlings an thrushes chatterin in the trees, magpies hoppin across the fields. That buzzard's back again, up above Pen Dinas, circling the summit. Lots of birds around today. Very few yesterday, tho; just a couple of spadgers an hoodies in the garden. What do all the birds do on such birdless days? What happens to them, I wonder? Maybe a soaring hawk or prowling cat or dog or stoat. Or maybe they all go an gather somewhere, the birds, gather in a secret wood somewhere an swap stories, teach each other new songs, discuss what it is an what it involves to be a bird in a human garden. Or exchange info about which houses leave out the best food. Which have the cruellest cat.

Rebecca liked birds. She loved birds. An once, she told me why; cos when she was a kid at her nan's she'd be surrounded by birds brought off the docks by her grandad – mynahs an budgies an lovebirds an finches an stuff all over the house, left to fly free an cack everywhere. Terrible noise as well. An this one time her grandad brought back a great big hawk in a hood, called the whole family into the kitchen an there he was with this friggin eagle on his wrist, soon as he took the hood off it shrieked an flew out thee open door. Never to be seen again, altho Rebecca kept lookin for it; said she laughed when, a few days later, the neighbour called round hysterical, said an eagle had carried off her dog, this yappy-yap fuckin chihuahua effort that kept Becca awake at nights. That pleased her. An from then on that's what she'd think of before she drifted off to sleep; of that eagle, magnificent exotic bird, soaring over the city, swoopin down across the pitch at Anfield an pooing all over Goodison. That's what Rebecca said.

Step 2: We came to believe that a power greater than ourselves could restore us to sanity. Any higher power; not necessarily God, altho for some that's inevitable, an if God then not necessarily an institutionalised depiction of It. It could be the sea; the sky; a specific tree; history. Anything that you could lose yerself in. Some would have to wait for that Higher Power to enter their lives unexpectedly, because searching for one would be pointless, and for those people that Higher Power could never be a person because that would assuredly lead to further destruction but it could be a book, a film, a place, a natural phenomenon, an animal; a fox, say, a one-eyed fox, come down off the mountain to sniff around yer garden while you watched it from the window, its utter ineffability so purely there in yer garden. An you watchin it. With what's left of yer left arm throbbin in yer empty sleeve an what's left of yer dignity mewling faintly in yer skull.

CAR

They enter Chester from the west, along Hoole Road. One of the newer areas of the city, which is to say that it lies some way outside the Roman walls and in the shadows of the sixties stacks and that if Roman stone or forgotten artefact, tool or tomb should appear here then it would do so in the manner of intrusion, blunting a blade digging out footings for some extension or interrupting the work of the cable layer. Arcane utensil or stone shaped by such demanding the delay of patio or laundry room or granny flat or new house entire. History itself barging through into business undifferent apart from the machinery corralled into its making it could all never be but one strong enterprise; the imprinting of human endeavour into the soil. And the clay. And even into the rock beneath that, black or red layers of earth and ash where and when whole cities were razed. Sunken strata struck with war.

Something is happening, or is about to happen, in the city, some footy match or show at the Arena because there are many people milling around the train station, a big crowd and rowdy. There is a conspicuous police presence too, some of them mounted, one horse being used to guard two yellow-jacketed officers who have thrown a lad over the bonnet of a car and are frisking him wrist to ankle. Darren slows the car down and crawls past this tableau.

—Look at these cunts, Ally. Mudderfuckers. Leave the lad alone, yis pairer fuckin pricks!

One of the friskers looks up at the car, a glare unwanted and Darren, mindful of the job he is on and the consequences should he fail in its execution, speeds up and away down on to City Road. Alastair murmurs something about missing the ring road but Darren either does not hear him or decides to unheed.

—Fuckin bizzies. Fuckin scum, lar, tellin yeh. Bad, bad scallies. Member them two that gave yis a kickin in the Copperas Hill bridewell? Member that? Scum of the fuckin earth, man. Gave yis a fuckin doin over two measly wraps a fuckin bugle. Never really recovered from that one, did yeh, kidder?

Alastair reaches up underneath his baseball hat to stroke a knotty lump there. Gone fibrous now and tough but still prominent. —Got three grand compo, tho, didn't I?

—Yeh, an stuck the fuckin lot of it straight up yer nose. Wrecked the few brain cells the fuckin jacks left intact.

He glances sideways at Alastair who continues to stare down at the road map spread on his knees. Darren regards the thin face, the weak chin and the downcast eyes, all this in the putty skin, and shakes his head. No expression on his face which can be easily read.

They cross a bridge, low over the canal. Sunlight skims off the green water into Darren's eyes.

—Aw for fuck's sakes. Near fuckin blinded me. Djer bring any shades with yeh, Ally?

Alastair shakes his head. —No. Forgot.

—What, yer dinner *and* yer fuckin gigs? Anythin yer fuckin *did* remember to bring?

—Brought *this*, didn't I? Alastair holds up the road map. —Woulden av a clue where to fuckin go if I hadn't've, would we?

—Yeh, so give me some friggin directions well. We're nearly in the city now, where do we go from here?

—Well, we're fucked for the ring road . . . but we're alright; we can go through the city centre. Turn right ere.

—Where?

Alastair points. —There. Under that big archway thingio.

Ancient gate through the ancient walls. Grand arch of the conqueror once sprouting heads severed and staked of the conspirative and seditious or just merely the Celt. Under the thin exhaust-soot skin these blocks bear scars, slices and scrapes and chippings and dents, a permanent war portal through and under which traffic chugs deliberate, designed as it has and will do. Hoof now rubber atop and compressing the stamp which continually swelters in layers excremental both dung and fume, gaseous and cacatic.

The vehicles move slow. Some kind of blockage on the road ahead.

—C'maaarrrn! Darren sounds the horn twice. —Move yer fuckin arses!

A passing pedestrian gives a disapproving look and Darren responds with a finger. —The fucker *you* lookin at, yeh ginger twat . . . See that cunt, Ally? See the fuckin kite on him? Ginger fuckin bastard.

He pronounces 'ginger' with hard g's, so that it rhymes with 'singer'. He scowls at the pedestrian's hurrying back.

—Yeh know what gets me, Ally?

—What's that?

—Why do ginger cunts never dye their friggin hair? I mean, there's an easy way out for them, like, isn't there? Paul fuckin Scholes, lar. If I was a friggin jinj I'd be *straight* down the chemist's, no messin. Get one a them home-dye jobs. I mean, it's not like thee need placcy fuckin surgery or anythin, is it? Few quid, that's all. Simple fuckin procedure. Slap it on yer ed, wait ten minutes, wash it off an there yer go: no more jinj. Easy.

Ally smiles. —Pure fuckin inconsiderate if yeh ask me.

—Is right, man, yeh. Inconsiderate. Selfish bastards.

The traffic moves. Edges forwards. A few cars peel off at a pelican crossing and Darren makes to follow them but the beacon peeps frantically as if crying to be fed and he must brake and wait while more people cross the road.

—Aw Jesus friggin Christ. Be all fuckin day at this rate. Urry up, yeh fuckin –

He stops abruptly. Staring through the windscreen at the crossing people, fixedly at a straggler, a young woman carrying a baby.

—Well, son of a cunt, look who it is.

—Where?

Darren points at this young woman with a chunky banana finger in a gleaming sovereign ring.

33

—*Her*, there. Look at the fuckin slag.

She is crossing the road slowly, this woman, auburn hair tied back, black boot-cut jeans low on her hips and a short black sleeveless bodywarmer, black T-shirt underneath. She has a baby strapped to her chest and she is pressing her lips to this child's fontanelle and holding it tight to her with one bare arm while in the other around a hooked finger she carries a clear plastic bag of big, bright oranges.

—Who is it?

—Fucks, Ally, don't yeh recognise her? It's that mad fuckin slut who strangled her fuckin boyfriend! Remember? The one who dissed us, dissed yeh in that Dock Road pub that night, bout a year ago? Last fuckin February or summin like that?

Ally shakes his head. Staring at the woman who has now stopped in the middle of the road to flusteredly adjust one of the straps around her waist that hold the baby to her body.

—Yeah, yer know! The one oo went out with Peter! She killed her boyfriend while thee were shaggin, strangled the poor cunt to death an she was fuckin knocked up by him. Didn't even serve any time, the murderin fuckin who-er.

Strap safely adjusted the young woman looks and smiles apologetically at the car coughing and grumbling by her. Her smile tugs at something in Alastair, some string or sinew which could be located in heart or groin or head or even neck, he doesn't know. He watches her cross and step on to the kerb. Darren winds his window down with big and angry arm movements and sticks his head out.

—Ey, you, murderin bitch!

The woman turns to face the car.

—Yeh, I'm talkin to *you*! Murderin fuckin bitch!

Only her eyes are visible over the top of her baby's head and those eyes swell wide.

—Fuckin killer! Strangled any more boyfriends lately? Fuckin psycho slag!

She spins away and drops the oranges and clutches the child tight to her and runs. Ponytail bouncing between her shoulder blades and the oranges bouncing off the kerb to land and roll in the gutter.

—Should be fuckin inside, you! Shoulda got fuckin lifed up! Fuckin bitch who-er!

People have begun to stare but Darren is oblivious, spitting words at the fleeing woman's shrinking back, Ally squinting at that woman through the Plexiglas and whatever his reaction to Darren's roared words and their context and intent cannot be read neither in that squint nor seated bearing nor the crane of his neck towards the car's side window and the ancient city in the world beyond that and the young woman with the infant running through it all, through the crowd of shoppers either openly staring or pointedly ignoring the sweaty head bellowing obscenities out of the car window.

—SLAG! MURDERER! FUCKIN KILLER!

A minibus overtakes, almost mounting the kerb, squashing the oranges in the gutter. Five flattened suns. The pressure-rips in their rind leaking juice almost fleshlike, muscular. And like subcutaneous fat, the white pith.

—Ey, Darren.

Alastair puts a hand on Darren's forearm and the large head contracts back inside the car and swings towards him. That face; the dark eyes flashing and the teeth gritted in the square jaw below the flared nostrils. Burst veins on the sides of that knuckled nose almost visibly throbbing.

—Berrer calm down, lar. Bizzies're fuckin all over the shop. Might hear, like. An anyway the light's gone green.

—Yeh, but for fuck's sakes.

Darren grinds the car into gear, drives on and away. Alastair points to a turning and Darren takes it.

—I mean, believe that shit, lar? Fuckin bitch wastes her own fuckin boyfriend, chokes the poor get to death an gets a suspended fuckin sentence. Shoulda been fuckin lifed up, the murderin fuckin slag. It was in thee *Echo* an everythin; death by misadventure. Misadfuckinventure!

He shakes his head. —Not fuckin right, that, man. I shit you not. That's the poor cunt's fuckin baby n all; fuckin slag, walkin round with a dead man's kid as if she's done fuck all. Nothin to be ashamed of. An the way she treated Peter . . . Honest to fuckin God.

—Daz, yer drivin too fast, mate. Fuckin place is crawlin with jacks. Slow down a bit, lar.

Darren does.

—Fuckin whore. Tell yeh what, tho; Peter'll be *well* friggin chuffed to find out where she's livin now, won't he? Oh yeh. Too fuckin right. Fact, I'm gunner call the cunt up *now*. Eeyar, pass us that fuckin moby, will yeh.

Alastair takes the mobile phone from the dashboard,

an Ericsson wrapped in a little PVC case as if in some kind of S & M play and hands it to Darren who takes it and taps in a number from memory with the thumb of his holding hand. Puts it to his ear.

—Switched off. Divvy. Don't know what he's missin.

He replaces the phone on the dash. —I'll try him again later. That fuckin whore.

Face pinked, excited and hectic, he turns to Alastair and grins. —Right, Ally. That's got me in the mood now. Let's go an welly this one-armed cunt.

—Alright. Didn't yeh wanner stop off somewhere first, tho?

—Oh aye, yeh. That fuckin post office. I'll need some directions. Where'd yer put that fuckin map?

They turn on to a bridge, cross the River Dee with the Queen's Park racecourse wide and green on their right. Some horses running and a packed mass of people watching them run. They pass too an amphitheatre, relatively well preserved behind railings the stone seating still intact and the pit now gravel for the tourists and archaeologists and historians and those given to whatever disciplines, any of which configuration must girdle the inanimate. And not in files or folders do women run and does blood spill and will power tumesce at torture but in streets and rooms and offices and their followers fond and fevered, traversing bewildered these hot grottos and mad galleries mortared with delirium, it's all just money changing hands and those reaching hands one mystery.

Chester gets smaller behind them. Wrexham gets bigger in front.

OFFICE

The Londis opposite the fire station has a small hoarding by its door advertising the local paper an the message on it is of thee imminent opening of a new call centre; 300 NEW JOBS FOR LOCAL COMMUNITY, it says. So I know, now, what they'll offer me in the DSS — a position in the modern sweatshop. Answerin the phones all fuckin day. 'A disability such as yours will be no hindrance in this type of work,' they'll say, all that fuckin nonsense. But which 'disability' will thee be referrin to? There's many, in me an on me. Not just me missin arm.

I'd probly fail the personnel test anyway, unless I play daft. Them kinds of places, the interviews an the tests an stuff, they're just designed to work out whether yer dim enough for the job, cos there's no way a work-force made up of lively imaginations would ever put up with forty hours of low-paid drudgery an tedium every friggin week. Most people, of course, *are* too bright for such jobs, but they get compelled into accepting them by the dreary demands of daily life, the usual financial imperatives. Which only ever results in one thing; a deep, deep, frustration. Disillusionment goin to impotence goin eventually to a terrible fuckin anger. Peter Salt, me caseworker in the rehab clinic, on one of the rare occasions when we conversed about somethin other than meself an me cravings, referred to this mental state as one of 'cognitive dissonance', meaning the dislocation we feel with arselves when we begin to behave in ways that drastically contradict ar self-image, such as that necessary alteration of behaviour demanded by certain jobs; in the case of the call centre, say, havin to talk politely to a hundred thousand disembodied voices when you're a naturally shy or at least not particularly garrulous person. Or havin to be polite to rude fuckers when all yer really wanner do is tell em to fuck right off. Yer forced to behave completely out of character, always, an it's awkward an unsettling an it just goes on an on, along with thee unrelieved monotony of the job itself. It's an awful fuckin state of affairs, an to counteract it, to give yerself some sort of renewed self-respect or empowerment or wharrever, yeh start to behave in petty an puerile ways; yer start stealin things from yer workplace or indulging in gossip or participating in the persecution of a workmate, all that stuff. The phrase 'cognitive dissonance' is a good one here; it suggests that yer mind doesn't rhyme, doesn't chime. Yer mind doesn't rhyme cos acting in these puerile ways begins to erode the sense you have of yerself as essentially a good an decent person. So yeh begin to dislike yerself. So yer mind stops rhyming cos then yeh try to make yerself feel better, more influential on yer surroundings, so yeh do things like stealing in an attempt to undercut those who have power over you. An so begins an endless cycle of pettiness, triviality. A world of the immature an inconsequential from which thee only real escape is to jack in yer job, walk out. Shite on

39

thee entire fuckin thing an go straight to the humiliation of the dole.

Or die.

Nice one.

An yer mind just stops rhyming. The *you*, the mental *you* won't slot together any more. Clanging an discordant an screeching yer new unrhymin mind.

An all their fuckin talk of 'choice' an 'opportunity' . . . yer arse. Such words are only used by those in the position to force an compel an make demands on others. Thee don't know the fuckin meaning. Thee haven't gorrer clue. For 'choice' read 'dilemma'. Read 'no viable way out'. Read 'do this an suffer or don't do this an suffer in a different way'.

Bastards. I'll friggin well *take* your disability benefit, yeh. You can live on disability benefit, not like income support or unemployment benefit; DB can keep you on top of yer bills an in food an fags. So there *is* a choice, then: lose a friggin limb. Get gangrened up from a broken spike an have the fuckin rotten thing lopped off like a bad branch on a tree.

'Cognitive dissonance' . . . a *good* phrase.

I see Shakey goin into the pub over the road by the bridge. Not to drink; to work. He's worked in almost every pub in this town, Shakey has, an there's plenty of em. Another Scouser who left the city to find somethin else, or because he couldn't safely remain there, like Colm. Like me. Like fuckin loads of us.

Shakey gives a wave an I wave back an he disappears round the back of the pub to the kitchens. I peer in the pub winda as I pass an I hear meself gasp an then quickly avert me eyes an speed up me pace focusing intently on the ground at me feet, flagstones small weeds glinting silica chips fag ends a chewy like a small pink brain but it's no good I cannot get rid the image lingers:

That dimmed light. An opaque maroon light womb-like an cool. Points of clean yellow brightness from the pumps at the bar an the few early drinkers at that bar, their relaxed and slouching shapes. First pint of the day. Straight vodka or whisky to steady the hands. The pure froth an the rising bubbles an the colour of it, the golden fuckin colour. That racing in the blood. Just a far-off thrum but gettin louder an all those hours ahead an where will you be at thee end of them? Where will they an the drink take you? Yer friends comin in at intervals or if not yer friends then strangers bringin new places to explore. Thee endless bevvy, never runnin out an the light dimmin outside as the day dies in that world away from you, removed from you, yer out of it in here on the stool at the bar a bottle in one hand an a cigarette in thee other an that buzz in yer head, oh God that fuckin *buzzzzzz*, you an the world separate an you so safe so warm so potentially dangerous. Everything opening up to let you in all of it so welcoming and

Jesus Christ. I fell to me knees in places like that. Wanted to as soon as I walked in them. Soon's I opened the fuckin door.

Up on to Trefechan Bridge. Wind in me face. Sounds of geese below. Slight tang of salt in that wind off the sea and

Me in that dark light amid the hundred and laughing people. How my heart heated an grew an that

41

wonderful whiff of stale beer an old tobacco an I am now followed by that scent whether here in the world or in my crippled memory I do not know but I can smell it so strong so seductive I think it's gunner come on me again me tongue dries yes I look at me watch me hands are shaking trembling as if in fever it is

10:45 this fuckin thirst this fuckin thirst taste of iron deep in the throat a terrible dryness in the tubes of me face behind me eyes me nose me lips so dry they will crack an shatter there is this taste there is this thirst me tongue curls like burnt plastic it is ash all ash inside me face this taste of ash oh God this taste nothing will dispel this taste except except just one just one just one wee one to remove this taste to take the vileness of this taste away to put the skin back on me tongue please 10:46 scratch me chin to hear the rasp should've shaved it rasps it crackles in me throat me gullet so dry it's scorched in the sun left out in the sun in some salt pan somewhere some desert foul an featureless skin bubblin dry as sand as rock as grass burnt brown an soil cracked parched is the word dyin of thirst dehy dehy-dration too little moisture for steam I will wither just one you cunt just one wee one oh God the taste I can taste it still that taste that taste what is this fuckin taste eatin me face this taste 10:47 biting at an nibblin on me lower lip me lips me teeth so fuckin dry it hurts me lips blisterin bubblin they will they will split an crack out along me whole fuckin face it will fall in two no blood will flow cos I am dry so dry I am filled with nowt but dust an salt just crumble I will baked like brick bite harder against this fuckin taste bite harder again draw some blood I can taste blood so swallow it greedy gulp it gulp it against this bastard fuckin taste gulp it down against it *drink* it 10:48 the dryness this desert this salt lake inside me so dry so dry so fuckin dry imagine bubbles on the tongue thee pop an pour thee pop an pour *remember* those bubbles on the tongue *have* those bubbles on the tongue thee pop an pour thee pop an pour release release from this dry hell this bleached this dry this cracked an wizened state shrivelled an shrunken all moisture gone I have eaten a mattress that's what this taste is twelve dry crackers I cannot speak I cannot swallow I cannot fucking breathe just one oh 10:49 the fuckin relief the release that drink would bring sighing in ecstasy in five minutes I could be this evil taste gone reblooded relifed refreshed oh refreshed that word torrents of it down my gullet under a waterfall gob wide open to gulp a sea of it a golden bubbling ocean plunge in swim gob stretched wide feel it irrigate every cell every fucking cell of my dry an screaming corpse this body this body of salt I cannot live so bled of juice so dry so dry so dry so 10:50 howling howling for one fuckin drink any fuckin drink this taste my God I need some fuckin thing to keep me alive to stop me turning to ash to bone two tons of salt I have eaten I cannot blink I have peanuts for eyes pebbles stones on a sunbaked beach unreached by the sea that sea in a glass catching the light the light in it I would drink the light the liquid I need I need fucking liquid need need need this need in me in me right in me lungs shrieking for a drink my palms they are 10:51 paper I flex my fingers hear rustling skin flakes of dandruff dry scalp scalp like sandpaper face like sandpaper splitting so dry ah fuck oh God just one drink one tiny sip to keep me alive to stop this gravel breezeblock sand salt need need need you fuckin you fuckin just one fuckin drink turn around now go back to the pub nothing exists but for this fucking need this screaming need this NEED NEED THIRST NEED THIRST NEED THIRST NEED THIRST NEED THIRST NEED THIRST NEED THIRST NEED THIRST THIRST THIRST THIRST THIRST this

10:52

Jesus fucking Christ.

That was a bad one. I nearly bleedin did it there.

Nearly fuckin caved in, didn't I?

Shite.

Oh God. That was the worst one for some time; a matter of years even. Christ.

Scurry now, straight to the nearest shop, carton of orange juice an a bottle of Pepsi. Open em before I've left the shop even an necked em both within a hundred yards, relief an release with every swallow. Feel meself inflate again, swell, that strange fuckin taste completely gone, impossible to recall in its horrible mixture of vileness and temptation. Impossible to recall now, aye, but not impossible to re-experience; it'll come back. Tomorrow or next month, it'll come back, I *know* it friggin will.

Yeh, an you also know that you'll beat the bastard again. Never fuckin surrender to it. Never fuckin give in.

Triumph. But hear the clashing in your mind. Yeh but:

How fuckin *strong* I am.

Go into the DSS, wait in the queue til I'm called. Could do this blinded. This fuckin routine.

—Who's next please?

I goes over to the desk. Sit down, slide me card across the table.

—Any work paid or unpaid since you last signed?

—No.

Funny how these attacks, these dry attacks, thee never affect me stump. It's like nothin exists except for me need an me thirst, not even thee arm I once had. I just don't remember it. It's like I'm almost whole again.

—How's the job search going?

—Restricted. I've only got one arm.

—I'm aware of that, but there are plenty of jobs suitable. Many local farmworkers who've lost limbs find they can happily make a change in their career plans. D'you know there's a new telephone exchange about to open?

—No.

Oh do tell. Feign interest. Which I do, convincingly, I mean I nod an murmur at what seems like appropriate moments, but I'm thinkin about that young lad that Peredur told me about, the one that came into his meeting all fucked up, an that prompts me to remember a similar occasion at the clinic when they brought in some bloke, holdin him up by thee arms like, some bloke in what was once a suit, his forehead just one open weeping wound an the stink off him almost friggin visible an his eyes so yellow an the scabs around his lips falling off like snow an thee propped him up at reception an he swayed an looked around at all of us wasted figures grinning in embarrassed envy an me with one sleeve flappin empty an he shouted at the top of his voice: 'If there's anything in this world better than booze then I want to fucking know about it! YES!'

I remember bein surprised at how posh his accent was. An I remember laughing as well. I couldn't help it. He just summed the whole sad an pathetic sorry thing up.

He didn't last long in the clinic, tho; signed himself out quicker than friggin *I* did. Soon's I was legally allowed to, that was me – fwit. Gone. Skedaddle. With less than me full complement of arms, like, but dry an glad as all fuck to be out of there. Too many alkies in them bleedin places.

—I mean, it doesn't have to be the end of your working life, y'know. I personally know of several clients who've had accidents such as yours and gone on to –

One thing I'm worried about tho; I shouldn't have sent that postcard to Quockie. Regret doin it now. Daft of me, it was. Whether it was symptomatic of the disease, this yearning to self-destruct, I don't know, but I sent it off during a period of deep an huge sadness, a close-to-the-edgeness, of near-lapse or 'near-slip' as the AA jargon has it. Some urge to make some connection to me past life. To that time when despite its boiling horrors I was truly fucking alive.

Wish I'd never done it. But it'll be alright. Fuck, I can survive anything. Wharrever shit or catastrophe gets chucked into me life, I can fuckin well survive it. I'll come through.

I sign me name, take thee application forms I'm offered, thank the lady an go back outside. Sky still greying; rain clouds approachin from the north. I chuck the forms into the nearest bin an head off to the doctor's.

Clatter, rattle. Clang bang.

Step 3: We made a decision to turn our will and our lives over to the care of God – as we understood Him. So what did we do, we surrendered arselves an ar responsibilities to a force which seems offended by innocence. To a force which we could deem responsible for the carnage of ar lives in the first place. To a force apparently unable or unwilling to alter or ameliorate the catalysts of that carnage and to which if we had ever felt thee urge to address it before was only to curse and beg.

So what a great fuckin idea THAT was.

—*What?* Alastair can't believe what he's just heard. —
Yeh reckon that Tommy's too *soft?*

Darren nods. All serious, eyes locked ahead staring
through the windscreen. Were his hands not holding
the wheel his arms would be crossed firm across his
chest.

—How the *fuck* djer work *that* one out?

Memories like wind through Alastair's head; of the
sound of bones breaking, of human voices begging.
Of skullbone bulging through split scalp and iron bars
and cricket bats whacking burst tomatoes on to flesh,
and Tommy above it all, over it all, engineering every
scream and squirt.

—I've just told yeh, avven I, he let that fuckin
Quockie cunt go. Me, I would've tied the cunt up,
stuck im in the boot as insurance. Then, if we find
out he's tellin us porkies like, we get the fuckin truth
out of him. *That's* the way to do it. Not just give the
cunt a kickin then lerrim leg it straight down to Lime
Street to the first train out of fuckin town.

—Is that what he's done, is it? Done one?

Darren shrugs. —Probly. Dunno. Just sayin that I
don't trust the twat, that's all.

—Yeh but Tommy . . .

—Is pure fuckin shiters of Snake Tong Tony. Which

is another fuckin thing; *I* would've tracked down Tony hisself, not the cunt's fuckin *nephew*. I mean, what's all that about? *Tony's* the one who fucked off with the bugle so *he's* the one yeh need to welly, knowmean? Sept Tommy hasn't got the fuckin arse to bounce in on the Chinks, has he? Pure fuckin shiters, man. No lie.

—But I heard he fucked off to Hong Kong.

—Who?

—Tony Tong. That's why –

—Who told yeh that? Tommy?

—Might've been.

—Nah, truth is, Tommy didn't even *look* for im. Couldn't be arsed. Too lazy or too fuckin scared. All's he did was get some of his boys, crap ones at that, Gozzy Squires an Lenny Reece an their dick'ed mates, to lift Quockie from some alehouse in Chinatown an take im down to the docks, some ahl warehouse like. Tommy's there, fuckin largin it, givin it all the Godfather shite, holds a blade to the mudderfucker's nose, tells him he's gunner lose it unless he makes good what his thievin cunt of an uncle ripped off.

—Were yis there?

—Course I was fuckin there, yeh. *I* was the one who tied the boy to the chair.

—Ah.

The Wrexham ring road takes them around and through parts of the Chester business park. Squat, colourless buildings separated by flat grassland, the whole estate ostensibly built on negative principles: strip human commerce of muck and mess, hammer it flat, hammer it bland unless the notion of allure mutates

49

in minds furrowed to the functional, the unadorned transactive. Unless the mountains distant and blue that fringe this plain far and haze-peaked massively lurking prompt of some movement alternative and particular oppositional to this place and the minds that made it cool and unsympathetic requisite of what they give, all renunciation of a life impassioned. What such programming can only ever give.

—Quockie's friggin cryin, beggin. Lookin at me like as if he knows me, the cunt, as if he's me fuckin bez or summin. Knew the twat at school, like, but . . . Darren shrugs. —That don't fucking change anythin; he's still gorrer fuckin rip-off merchant for a fuckin uncle. What does he expect me to do? Lerrim go cos we sagged a few classes together? Fucks.

Darren falls quiet as if in thought. Alastair prompts him.

—So what happened?

—When?

—With Tony's nephew. Quackie.

—Quockie. Don't yeh know? Tommy didn't tell yeh any of this, no?

—Not really, no. Just gave me this job like, said you'd clue me in.

—So yeh don't even know why yer in this fucking car with me, drivin inter fuckin Wales?

Alastair shakes his head. —Nah, not really. Just said to go along with you, like, said you'd clue me in.

—Jesus wept, Ally.

—Know it's got summin to do with a one-armed feller, like, that's about it.

Darren looks at Alastair briefly then snorts and nods

as if confirming something. Some inkling. Then faces front again and continues.

—This Quockie's got no money, there's fuck all he can do. So he gives Tommy some info instead like, dunny. See, three, four years ago, summin like that, bit less maybe, this fuckin alky screwed Tommy out of a loader swag an fuckin disappeared, fuck knows where. Mugged one of Tommy's little mules or somethin. Twelve years old like, believe that shit? Anyway, fuckin Tommy's been fucking tampin about this ever fuckin since. Turns out that this fuckin Quockie knew this cunt an recently got a postcard off him from this friggin place in Wales we're goin to.

—This is the feller with one arm, yeh?

—Is right. Lost it to gangrene or summin. Fuckin junkie, fuckin alky, likes. So Quockie tells Tommy where he thinks this stumpy mudderfucker might be hidin, Tommy says that'll do, gives the cunt a kickin an lets im fuckin go. Which *I* wouldna fuckin done, no messin. In the first fuckin place it wouldna been him tied to the fuckin chair, it would a been his tea-leaf fuckin uncle, the *real* rip-off bastard. Tellin yeh; Tong or no fuckin Tong, cunt would a been chained to that bleedin chair. Or if not that, if I couldna found him, like, I wouldn't've let tha fuckin Quockie go. No way. He'd be with us, here, in this friggin car. In the fuckin boot, lar.

A six-foot bronze trout, green with verdigris, leaps from a small shallow brown pond at the edge of the road, behind it some beige brick box with smoked-glass windows. Alastair regards that giant frozen fish as they pass.

—So that's us, Darren shrugs. —Here we fuckin are. In some fucked-up ahl shed of a car drivin inter fuckin Wales to look for some cunt with one arm when I could be kickin back in Sevvy Park with a spliff an a few tinnies.

He shakes his head and lets breath out through clenched teeth. —Fucking shite. Still n all tho, it's a ton for a day's work.

—If we find him.

—If we fuckin find him, yeh. Still fifty nicker if we don't, tho. But we will.

—Yeh. An Tommy said he'd chuck in another ton if we find that other musher.

—Who?

—Yer know. That other one who ripped him off. What's his friggin name now . . . Alastair takes a scrap of paper from his trackie pocket and consults the scribbles on it. —Downey.

—Oh aye, yeh, Downey. He ripped *Joey* off, not Tommy. T's just doin a favour for his brudder like cos Joey's in Spain at the mo. Met that cunt once, that Downey. Fuckin gobshite.

—Djer remember wharry looks like? Would yeh recognise him again?

—Dunno. Just look out for some mouthy fuckin no-mark shoutin the friggin odds an he's ar man. Gobshite, tellin yeh. Another friggin rip-off merchant. Sort *that* cunt out n all, lar, tell yeh.

Alastair crumples the paper back into his pocket and lights a cigarette. Darren reaches and takes it from his mouth and begins to smoke it instead.

—Oi! I've only got two left!

—Buy some more soon well. We'll be stoppin off in a bit.

—Yeh but fuckin hell, Darren. Yeh should've friggin asked.

—Shoulda fuckin offered, yeh tight-arsed get.

Mumbling Alastair grumbling Alastair lights another. Smokes it staring out at the far mountains getting closer growing larger blowing smoke out of his nostrils dragon-like or as if some embers burn inside him, as if some flame has been fed with smoke-producing fuel, some green grass or leaf or twig, any vegetable thing both young and green.

He takes his baseball cap off, scratches his head shaved to stubble then replaces it again. Winds the window down and flicks the cigarette end out where it is whipped instantly into the slipstream then winds the window up again.

—Tell yeh what, tho, Da.

—What's that, mate?

—I can't bump anyone. I don't have it in me to waste anyone.

—Who the fuck said yeh gunner have to? Who said a fuckin word about smokin anyone?

—No one did, like. It's just . . .

—We just do the knees or summin, that's all. This one-armed divvy, we'll just do one of his legs, like. Balance him out, knowmean?

Darren smiles but it is not returned.

—I couldn't waste anyone, Da.

—Well, yer not gunner have to. Just gunner say boo, that's all.

—Good, cos I couldn't.

—Yeh don't fuckin *have* to, man. Now fuckin less it, will yis? Shurrup about it now, ey, cos yer gettin right on me friggin nerves.

Darren's foot jerks involuntarily and the engine screams. There is a tiny spurt of speed from the car but nothing more.

—Christ, this fuckin car . . . gorrer have a word with Tommy when we get back, lar. Takin the friggin piss.

They pass a sign: RHOSLLANERCHRUGOG and an arrow to the right. Darren points.

—Look at this shit. How the *fuck* are yeh supposed to say that, eh? What kinder fuckin language is tha?

—It's Welsh, yeh div. Alastair points at another sign: a stylised dragon and CROESO I CYMRU. —Look, we're in Wales.

—I *know* it's fuckin Welsh, yeh knob. I *do* know what fuckin country I'm in.

—Well then.

—I'm just sayin that it's a mad fuckin language, that's all. I mean, how the fuck djer pronounce that? Crows-o aye Kim-roo? Fuckin stupid. Speak fuckin English. The fuck does it mean anyway?

Alastair is about to offer the correct pronunciation and definition of the welcome sign but his attention is diverted by a large fly, stripy of thorax, that whines into the car through the open vent on Darren's side. It lands on the dashboard. Darren notices it too.

—Jeez, look at the size of that bastard. Sliker fuckin bluebottle on 'roids.

As if at the sound of Darren's voice the fly turns

in three jerks to face him. Jerks thrice away from the window to face the driver.

—It's a cleg fly.

—Don't care wharrit's called. Orrible little get. He's gettin fuckin squashed.

Darren takes one hand off the wheel to crush the fly with his thumb.

—Nah don't, Da, it might –

—Aargh, yeh little cunt!

In a second the insect has leapt and bit and flown fed and whining away. The car swerves.

—Look at that! Cunt's drawn fuckin blood!

—I told yeh, didn't I? It was a cleg fly. Thee bite.

—Thanks for fuckin tellin me *now* like, when av just been friggin bit. Jesus fuckin Christ.

The car swerves again. Darren straightens it then turns his hand on the wheel to study the wound. Raised lump angry red like a boil. Small puncture in the centre of it leaking a thick little trickle of crimson blood.

—Be wrecked now, that fly. All the charlie that's in yer bloodstream, he'll be avin a great fuckin time.

—Jesus fuckin Christ, Darren repeats, glancing from the road to his hand then back again. —Look at that.

Alastair almost smiles. Darren licks the bite then replaces his hand on the wheel and looks out at the earth swelling, beginning to bulge it is into mounds and hills then higher still into mountains dark shadows streaking across them as the weak sun is gulped by cloud and ancient earthworks between which the road cuts and these formations millennia-old still huge still solid unbudgeable bulwarks against which any human movement could smash, shatter, lie sundered and torn. Unbroken by the endless weathering centuries withering of all else as if they could care. As if they could assist any flicker or twitch of the soft life within the moving metal so far at the base below that it could effectively *be* the base, unnoticed, some quick busy flickering so far below.

—Tellin yeh, Ally. Darren shakes his head. —Don't like this fuckin place, lar. This fuckin country. Never fuckin av. Fuller fuckin woollybacks, sheepshaggers. They're fuckin, thee've been fuckin left behind. Still fuckin sacrificin their kids to the fuckin sun-god n stuff, I shit you not.

Alastair laughs.

—No, it's true, am fuckin tellin yeh. Yer've only gorrer look at Lenny Reece, fuckin balloonhead Lenny; he's from this area and he's off his fuckin tree. I mean, a place with this many mountains an lakes an woods, it's just not fuckin right. Fuckin witches n all sorts out here. Creepiest fuckin place. Does me fuckin head in. Just don't fuckin like it, lar. Don't fuckin like it. Wanner be back in town. Sooner we're outer the fuckin place the better. Fuckin tell yeh.

—Eeyar. Turn down there.

Alastair points to a road and Darren takes it.

—An this'll take us on to that postie, yeh?

—Yeh. That's where yeh wanner go first, innit?

—Yeh.

—That's where we're headin for, well.

—Good. I'm glad.

—Well, I'm glad that yer glad.

—Oh fuck off.

They drive into a village.

—Is this it? This is the place, yeh?

—Nah. Alastair shakes his head. —Next one.

—How djer know?

—Cos I'm readin the bleedin map, arn I?

—Yeh but you're thick, tho. We're probly in fuckin Scotland or somewhere.

—I'm tellin yeh it's the next friggin village. Says so on the map. An anyway I know cos I used to come on me jollies round ere as a kid, visitin me nan an that.

—Yer nan?

—Yeh. She was from Wales.

—She was Irish, lar. I met her one time, member, at that weddin? When there was that boss big brawl?

—That was me *dad's* mum. I'm talkin on me ma's side now.

—Ah. So yer've got woolly fuckin blood then? Explains a fuck of a lot, that, Ally. One *fuck* of a lot.

—No, I mean it. She was in service, like. Then when she got old she moved back to Wales. Her mam before her as well, y'know, for the rich cunts like? In Tocky an that?

—Tocky? No rich cunts in Tocky, lar.

—There was *then*. All them great big houses useter be owned by single families, did yeh know tha? Weren't flats or anythin *then*, Da. Just great big fuckin houses. Slave owners an ship owners an tha. Useter be a well-rich place, L8 did.

—An that's where yer nan worked?

—Yeh.

—An she was Welsh?

—Yeh. Spoke the language an everythin. That's how come I can speak all these place names, like. Useter teach me, she did.

—Well, as I say – explains one fuck of a lot, that, Alastair. I shit you not, lar, a lot of stuff's clear in me head, now.

Alastair shrugs. —Don't care.

—Oh yeh big soft get.

—No, just don't care what yeh think. About me nan or anythin.

—Yeh great big fuckin puff. Yeh gunner get all sulky on me now just cos I said tha?

Alastair shrugs again and does not answer and Darren makes an exasperated noise and they enter another village, little more than a hamlet, a handful of old stone whitewashed houses and a general store/post office. Characterised by leaf and bark, this small place built among trees, a forest once large. Shadow and harbour and hiding place and anchorage and sanctuary.

—There's the place, Ally, look. That's the one we're gunner screw.

—What, now?

—No not friggin *now*, softlad. On the way back.

—But it's titchy. There'll be fuck all there.

Darren turns into a small parking space overhung by branches in which gloom the car's colour becomes nameless, simply dark. Any anonymous old car making a stop on a journey.

—I told yeh before, didn't I? These houses round here're worth a fuckin fortune, man. They're all rich cunts' retirement homes like, or fuckin holidee homes. No bank for fuckin miles like, so thee all use that one

58

fuckin postie. Tell yeh, the safe in there'll be fuckin chocka. Muchos swag. Piecer piss n all – see? Only one ahl biddy workin in there. Place's friggin *screamin* to be screwed, lar. We'll be brewstered.

Darren turns the key and the engine dies. There is wind and birdsong. Some weak patters of rain on the roof, just a few spots. They look across the road at the shop and Alastair gazes behind that shop to where the green ground slopes skywards and gathers in a surge arrested into a vast and sheep-specked mountain mist-draped at the pinnacle as if that cloud in some unimaginable suction has slurped the earth up into one immense straining cone.

Darren elbows Alastair in the ribs. —Goan check it out, Ally.

—What?

—Go check it out, lar. Go an buy somethin an case the fuckin place while yer doing it. Scan the layout an tha. Thought yis needed some ciggies anyway.

—She'll see me face.

—So?

—So she'll recognise me later, like, won't she? When we rob it.

—Wrap somethin round yer head or somethin then.

—Oh, an that's not gunner look fuckin suspicious, is it? Goin in for some fags wither fuckin scarf tied round me face. Fuckin nice one, Darren.

—Not fuckin *now*, yeh knob'ed, *later*. Disguise yerself fuckin *later*.

—Oh yeh. Alright.

—Thick as shite, aren't yeh? Thick as fuckin pigshit, in that right?

—No.

—Go on then, gerrin there, well.

Darren is pushing Alastair towards the door.

—Djer want anythin?

—No. Just fuckin gerrin there.

Push push.

—Some sweets or anythin? I mean –

—FUCKIN GERRIN THERE, ALASTAIR!

Darren opens the door on Alastair's side and shoves him out and slams the door shut. He watches Ally stand and brush his trackie down then look left and right at the kerb and watches him cross the road and enter the small shop. He hears the faint double 'ting' as the door opens and closes and watches through two sheets of glass, the windscreen and the shop window, as the old lady proprietor stands behind the counter smiling and saying something to Alastair as he hands her some purchases and she takes them and rings them into the till. Then Alastair darts behind the counter with her and she drops floorwards.

—Fuck! Mad bastard's gunner screw it *now*! Shite!

He punches the dashboard then leaves the car in a rushed muddle. He bangs his hip on the headlight and hisses then passes in an urgent jog the bonnet and crosses the road without looking and jogs towards the shop. A fat and full cleg fly crawls sluggishly across the inside of the windscreen and down on to the dash where it flexes its wings and rubs its forelegs together as if in glee then cleans its bulging eyes with those same bristled limbs then jerks through 360 degrees as if searching for something then disappears slow and sated through a vent hole in the dash. Small gluttonous vampire taking bloodbooty into hiding. Seeking that darkness in which to digest away from larger carnivores its sustenance and victual down somewhere into oil-drip cranny, secret sheened bolthole. The cooling engine ticks and nickers, murmurs and gurgles faintly, each dull tick the tap of a hammer chipping away at, sculpting the hush.

Two tracksuited figures move towards the car. One is carrying a brown paper bag, the other, larger one is gesticulating all angry with both big hands, brass-knuckled with sovereigns. Their voices swell proportionate with their shapes as they approach the car and loom over the bonnet and enter the vehicle separately, one to each side.

—. . . mean, I thought yeh were gunner skank the place there an fuckin then! The *fuck* were yeh doin, lad?

—Ahl queen dropped me change, that's all. I was just helpin her pick it up.

—Yeh, well, yerra soft fuckin twat. Useless fuckin cunt, you.

The engine splutters into life.

—How? How am I a cunt?

—Cos she's seen ar fuckin grids now, hasn't she? Eh? Knows what we fuckin look like now, doesn't she? Honest to fuckin God.

Darren shoves the car into gear and pulls back on to the road as fast as the old tired engine will allow.

—Yeh, well, yeh didn't have to come bargin in like that, did yeh? Made it look dead fuckin obvious like, that did.

—Fuck off, Alastair.

—Thought you said we were gunner wear masks anyway?

—Got no fuckin choice now, av we? Fuckin dick'ed you, Alastair. Honest to God. Fucked everythin now you av. Cunt.

Wordlessly Alastair takes a box of fudge out of the paper bag and rests it on his knees. Looks down at it, at the picture on the lid of the whitewashed cottage on the hillside by the lake which reminds him of the house in which his grandmother lived as the shopkeeper with her specs and accent reminded him of his grandmother herself. He opens the box, offers it to Darren who hisses and shakes his head so Alastair withdraws the offer and begins to eat the fudge, lots of it, barely chewing, letting it dissolve into sweet and sticky film in his mouth. Gazing out the window.

The mobile phone rings: 'You'll Never Walk Alone' ring tone. Darren snatches it up, reads the display and puts it to his ear.

—Yeh, Tommy . . . nah, still fuckin miles away . . . hasn't gorrer fuckin clue . . . nah . . . alright, yeh . . . ey, have yeh seen Peter? Peter the Beak? . . . tell him to give me a bell fuckin soon as, will yeh? . . . alright, well . . . yeh . . . no problemo . . . nah, I'm gunner turn it off for a bit cos the battery's runnin low . . . he can leave a fuckin voicemail . . . I'll call *you* . . . yeh . . . laters, Tommy.

He turns the mobile off, tosses it over his shoulder on to the back seat.

—What did –

—Shurrup, Alastair. Don't say another fuckin word

for the next ten minutes cos I'll probly fuckin snot yis.

Alastair falls, and remains for some time, silent. Just the car's grumbling engine labouring and the slurping in his ears as he sucks and devours fudge.

DOCTOR'S

Don't know why it is, like, but the waitin room in this surgery, the Church Surgery like, is always full of fit women. Don't mean fit as in healthy – if thee were fit in that way thee wouldn't be here in the friggin doctor's, would thee? – I mean fit as in sexy, attractive. That one over there by the yucca plant with the dark hair and dark skin, readin a book. She's friggin gorgeous. Cool, as well; all aloof to them crusties around her, must be script day for em, she's just gettin on with her readin an waitin as if thee mean nowt to her. Shakin like a shittin dog, one of em is – jactitation, the compulsive twitchin, like, altho the holes he's scratchin in his yellowed arms are more to do with the bile salts accumulating in his skin that his failin liver's released, turnin him that horrible jaundiced shade. Pigments of bile. Early stages of cirrhosis. Not long to go, poor fucker. Get out of it while yer can, lad. But I know yeh won't.

So familiar to me, these places are, the waiting rooms in doctors' surgeries. Spent so much time in them I did when I was seein Rebecca, hangin round them, pacin the floors, itchin to get ar hands on temazzy scripts or other stuff we could blag that we'd sell on to buy bevvy or use arselves to make the bevvy we *could* afford go further. Temazepam turns lager into whisky, too right. So many hours spent in these places, these drab an dull places full of sick people. Thee associative memories are of frustration, sweat, need, thirst, a vile dry torture. Me an Rebecca snappin at each other, snarlin at each other. An all thee other abusers around us, junkies leaking, alkies dripping. Terrible fuckin days. I see these people around me here in the same state now as I was then an it makes me

it makes me

only disconnect

Some voice is callin me name. I snap out of the trance an evryone in the waitin room's lookin at me except the cool pretty girl an the lady behind the counter's smilin at me an holdin me notes out towards me an she calls me name again. I smile an step up to the counter an take me notes off her. A big, thick bundle.

—Dr Hoek, last door on the left down the corridoor.

—Ta.

So peaceful, them trances. Nothin but my body, no past, no future, no memories, no world. Just me an my heartbeat. An utter nullification, complete egodeath an nowt but pure peace. Wonderful. Wish thee could last for ever.

I knock on the door. A nice feller, Dr Hoek; Dutch, I think. Nice bloke. Isn't that the name of the dog in *Ren & Stimpy*? Yeh, I think it is. Ren Hoek. He calls for me to go in an I do.

—How are you?

—Alright, I say. —Not bad.

I give him me notes an he flicks through them.

65

—No problems? No pain or itching?

—In me arm, yeh mean?

—Yes.

—No.

—Any bad smells or redness?

—No. It's fine. Apart from being only half there, like.

He smiles. —Let's have a look then. Take your top off please.

I grab me fleece at the collar an pull it up over me head. Me half-arm lifts and reaches, wantin to help like, but it only creates an obstacle so I have to consciously will it to remain still an submissive as I tug the fleece off over it. Static electricity crackles in me ears an I can feel me hair standin on end. I smooth it down with me palm an rest me fleece on me knee an Dr Hoek slides on his chair towards me for a closer look.

—Let me see.

I raise me stump towards him. Me eyes suddenly heat up an I want to cry; it can get me like this, on occasion, all quick an unexpected, how pathetic it looks sometimes all abbreviated an feeble as if it's not part of me but some terribly vulnerable an ill-equipped thing. A thing essentially good an gentle but doomed to suffer horribly precisely because of those qualities. Thee end of it, smooth an blank, all features obliterated by suffering.

No, shurrup, don't be fuckin daft. It's you. It's you. This thing is not separate, it is a part of *you*. And now it always fuckin well *will* be.

—Mmmm . . . healing very nicely this is . . .

He's prodding it, softly an carefully. Runnin his thumb along the barely noticeable scar, the pale, raised seam where the flaps of skin were stitched together.

—Heck of a good job, this . . . beautiful . . .

Ah, that's nice; he called me half-an-arm 'beautiful'. How sweet. What an interesting mind you have, Dr Hoek.

Over his shoulder I can see the top of his desk. His screensaver's of moving stars, as if you're hurtlin through space. Not very calming for a doctor's office. There's a golfing trophy and two photographs, one of a woman in a headscarf and shades smiling and thee other of two children grinning on a beach with a sea behind them and an empty mug next to that and in a blue glass vase there's a bunch of flowers, yellow flowers, daffodils I think thee are, little yellow trumpets an thee look an I bet thee smell

stinkmushrotdecayitfallsawaywefallaway

nice.

He clasps thee end of my arm in his palm and squeezes.

—Does that hurt?

—No.

He squeezes harder. —That?

—No.

An it doesn't, it doesn't hurt, but it feels a wee bit odd an uncomfortable like a mild electric pulse an it makes me wisdom teeth throb an I want him to stop squeezing an he does.

—Okay then. No problems. I'll write you out for some more codeine. You can get dressed now.

He scribbles on his pad an I struggle back into me

fleece. An it *is* a struggle; try gettin a fleece over yer head with only one fuckin arm. Should've worn a shirt, shirts are easy, but with fleeces you have to roll the friggin thing up into some semblance of a hoop an put it over yer head an somehow worm yer whole arm into the sleeve then take thee empty sleeve an bunch it up an then kind of roll it up over yer half-arm like a giant woolly condom. It's not easy. An then pin thee empty sleeve up or tuck it into the waistband of yer kex like I do now to stop it friggin flappin about everywhere all empty. Pain in the fuckin arse, to say the friggin least.

But it's *you* now. It's just one of the things yeh do like sleepin an eatin an showerin an tryin to cook one-handedly. It's just you. It's what goes towards makin you whole.

—Here you go.

He hands me the script an I tuck it into me breast pocket. I'll hand it in at Boots an I can pick up the pills tomorrow; I'm not in dire need of them just yet, I haven't run out. So it can wait.

—Is there anything else?

—What, yeh mean drugs?

—No, no, I mean, there's no other problems? Everything else okay?

I shrug. —Yeh. Suppose. Why?

—You're sleeping well?

—Mostly, aye. Sometimes I find it difficult to drop off, like, but . . .

—Nightmares?

—Who doesn't?

—Every night?

—Oh no.

—How often?

—What, thee insomnia or the bad dreams?

—The insomnia.

—Couple a times a week or so, that's all. It's not a problem, honest.

—What about in here? He taps his temple twice. —How are things in here?

What a mad question. How the fuck am I supposed to reply to that? Thee accurate answer would simply be a list of about eight hundred adjectives an then some kind of cohesive exegesis attempting to explain that the prevailing condition inside my skull is one strangely, paradoxically, of wholeness. Despite loss an sadness an horror an rot an desultoriness an drifting an rage an pain, it's really one of wholeness.

—Fine. I shrug an smile. —I'm happy, in general.

—Good. He smiles as well an turns back to me notes. —Your records. You erm, you detoxed in . . . where was it?

—St Helens.

—St Helens.

—On a DTTO.

—On a Drug Treatment and Testing Order, that's right. And it worked for you?

—Yeh.

—Urges? Cravings?

—Well, yeh, of course, but . . .

—I've been doing some reading on addiction, he says. —One doctor, it's in Australia I think, has discovered that a craving, an urge in addicts, lasts anything between nine seconds and six minutes. So, if you can fight it for seven minutes, you're going to be okay. Seven minutes.

I smile. —Seems about right.

—I know it must seem like a long time, seven minutes.

—I can manage, tho. I'm strong.

—Good. I'm glad to hear of it.

—Clean an serene, that's me.

We both smile an the stupid fuckin Serenity Prayer runs by rote through me head again, that daft fuckin Serenity nitwit Prayer: 'God grant me the serenity to accept the things I cannot change, courage to change the things I can, and the wisdom to know the difference.' Oh yeh, an also, 'Grant me the self-knowledge to be aware that this prayer is a reductive an simplistic load of bollox, a mere an empty New Agey bullshit index to another form of obsessive behaviour in the Twelve-Step Programme to which we must all rigidly adhere in a manner that suggests that, if we don't surrender the few brain cells the drink and drugs have left us with, then we are nothing but blemishes on the planet, stains, life unworthy of life.'

Arse. Well done, One-arm. We love you, One-arm. You're worth it you're worth it you're worth it.

Arse.

—Tell me something, the good doctor says. —Have you thought about a prosthetic?

I think about it, back home in the bottom of me cupboard; me shiny placcy arm. Sort of creepy. —I've already got one, I say.

—And you choose not to wear it?

—Yeh.

70

—Can I ask why?

—Well, for one, it's kind of uncomfortable. It rubs, like. An it just doesn't feel right; it's like I'm carryin a weight around with me when I wear it. An awkward weight? Like a rucksack full of bricks or summin?

He nods.

—It's like I feel kind of incomplete with it on, djer know what I mean? Like, y'know, it's just not me. It's an additive, something imposed on me from without. It's not me. I'd sooner feel whole, like. Complete.

—It would've been easier, I think, for you if the cut had happened below the elbow. Prosthetics are a lot better with that hinge to work on, you see?

He flexes his arm a few times at the elbow.

I shrug. —I don't think it would've made any difference, to be honest with yeh. Still sooner do without.

He nods and smiles, as if pleased at my words. God knows why, like. Bit odd, Dr Hoek.

—Okay then. I'll see you in, what, two weeks?

—Two weeks, yep.

—Make an appointment on your way out at reception. Glad to see you're well.

—Ta.

I leave an go back into the waiting room. The pretty girl's gone, the crusties've gone. Just a few ahl biddies, singly or in couples, one couple with the reddest faces I've ever seen talking heatedly at each other in Welsh. I take me one an a half arms up to the counter to make a date an time for me to come back here again for a prodding.

71

Step 4: We made a searching and fearless inventory of ourselves. And no matter how fearless we thought we were, such an inventory took us nowhere near as far into the black pits of ar hearts that drugs took us to, that drink took us to. We took some wimpy an tentative steps into those vile places an we thought an were told that we were showing bravery an were encouraged, praised an patted, yet we were fucking cowards, pure cowards cringing compared to what we were when we danced an laughed in a conga line as we waved goodbye to every last limp shred of innocence. Tara, we said. See ya.

CAR

Under a sky gunmetal and between green surgings large enough to scrape that sky they drive deeper, further into Wales. The old and grinding engine, the whine and clank of it bouncing off the leaping earth.

—Still got a cob on, Da?

Deeper, further into this country, lakes the same slaty shade as the clouds above and the mountains granite-spurred and serrated on the flanks as if gnawed by some massive maw and the valleys between them sucking the eye through the deep troughs to where other swellings equal destabilise greyly the horizon, ripple and peak and spike and sawtooth the grey horizon and beyond that still and always the same sight repeated, repeated to the abrupt escarpment of the sea at which this labouring car and the two inside it are aimed. Once fortresses now hills, some of these huge humps were. Defensive earthworks now a rambler's challenge through which the small car chugs with purpose, intent.

—Da. You still cobby, mate?

And nomads of quite another order, these two in this car are. Nothing in them or their quest of truth or beauty nor justice morality or law but of some species of warfare of a sort that is played out on the outer peaks or in the roots of the wind-twisted trees

73

bent arthritically earthwards. Gnash in this landscape, slash in this landscape tooth and talon on and in always this hard landscape once soft and gouged by claw or by flesh inured enough to have too been claw. From ravenous rippings in the pocks and pits of the soil too thin here to sustain growth other than that which from these buried feedings became the hacking hand of man and rocks ripped out and shaped and stacked to form a fortress both protection from and site from which to propel still more flesh-render, surrender and submit, to the screeching machines which shred the sky hourly and somewhere within this history unending this small farting automobile spluttering smoke and the faulty flesh-weapons, launched torpedoes of skin and bone inside it.

—Darren.

—What?

—Yeh still narky? Still got thee arse?

Darren shakes his head.

—Then why the friggin deadhead, lar? I mean, yer've been blankin me since –

—Oh shut yer fuckin gob will yeh, an giz a piecer that fudge.

Darren takes with his left hand some fudge, three pieces, from the open box on Alastair's knee and crams all three into his mouth. Already plump cheeks bulge hamsterly as he chews and his face scrunches like a paper bag as he gulps.

—Fuck me, lar. Fuckin hangin, that is. Pure disgustin. So fuckin *sweet*, Jesus.

Alastair eats some also. —Well, I like it.

—It's just fuckin sugar, y'know, that's all it is, pure

sugar boiled up with a drop of milk. Might as well have just bought a fuckin bag of Tate an Lyle, I shit yis not. Et the fuckin stuff wither spoon.

—Just wanted summin sweet, didn't I?

—What, after that bag of Sayer's doughnuts yer ad for yer brekkie when we were still in town? Gunner fuckin cark it before yer thirty, you, all that sugar. Arteries like iron bars.

—Don't remember seein *you* refuse any.

—No cos I was starvin, wasn't I?

—You ate four of the fuckers. Four to my two.

—Yeh cos I was Lee fuckin Marvin! Last thing I ate was that bag of jockeys on, when was it, night before last. Fuckin belly thinks me throat's been cut. To be honest, I could go *more* of them friggin dough-nuts. Bleedin starvin here I am. Could eat a scabby ed.

Alastair points at a large flat of dull-glinting dark water ahead of them between two gatepost hills. A small town hunched at the far end of it like huddled rushes, some freshwater vegetation as if sprouted natural from that lake from the ooze and the silt and the ice-black water itself.

—Eeyar. Stop off at Bala, well.

—Will there be a chipper or summin there?

—Oh yeh. A few, probly.

—Alright, well.

They pass between the mountains and on to the lake road. Furrow-browed with thought, Darren speaks:

—Have yeh ever thought, Ally, about what fat slob of a cunt invented the fuckin doughnut? I mean, what

75

was the blob thinkin? I know, let's get a ball of lard, deep-fry it in more fuckin lard, cover it with fuckin sugar an then inject it full of jam! I mean, what fat *fucker* thought that one up, ey? Probly someone who didn't fuckin live very long.

—Taste good, tho.

—Yeh, thee taste nice. Is right.

Alastair nods at the passing water. —Meant to be a monster in that lake, y'know.

—Is thee? What kind of monster?

—Dunno. Just a monster.

—A Nessie kind of feller?

—Dunno. When I was fishin there as a kid I met this Yank musher who was lookin for it. Said he'd spoken to someone who'd seen it an reckoned it looked like a crocodile with long legs.

Darren raises one eyebrow sceptical.

—I shit you not, Da. That's wharry said.

Darren snorts sceptical.

—Honest, Da, no messin. There's some funny fuckin things in that lake, I'm tellin yeh.

—Aye, I fuckin bet there is. Things the fuckin woolies'd chuck in there, Jesus. Sacrificin virgins an babies to the lake monster n all sorts.

—No, I mean it. Like, there's a fish in that lake that yeh can't find anywhere else in the world.

—Yer arse.

—No, it's fuckin true. I'm tellin yeh.

—Oh aye? What's it's fuckin name then, this fish?

—The gwyniad.

—Fuck off, you. Yer makin it up.

—I'm not, honest. That's thee only place in the

76

world yeh can find it, Bala Lake. Honest to God. Me grandad caught one once. Et it an everythin.

—Et it?

—Yeh. *Et* it.

—Was it gutted? Or just a bit pissed off?

Darren laughs loud at his own joke and Alastair smiles weakly either not quite comprehending it or not really hearing it, recalling as he is very strongly his grandfather at the edge of that plain of dark water casting the line out into it or reeling that same line in again and the excitement in Alastair as he watched the fighting fish churn the water or eel or whatever be drawn closer to the land and his own restless feet. Recalling the perch that he himself caught, the iridescent tiger stripes on its muscled flanks and the deep-black Vs against the glittering green scutellation and the sharp spines of its fins that punctured his palms when he tried to hold it tightly to arrest its wriggling for a trophy photograph. Or recalling the basking viper he disturbed beneath the branches of a willow he'd crawled under to take a shit and the way it thrashed and whipped into the water to flee him but not before he'd registered its flickering tongue and its fierce face with the peppercorn eyes and the black patterning on its back like an X-ray image of its own skeleton, that chain of dark arrowheads atop the shimmering grey scaling. Its face he recalls most clearly, the tongue and the eyes, and the utterly alien way it moved, some bayonet invested with a life and a venom too intense and taut to dwell upon. Twenty years ago and that face still scanned in his dreams.

They skirt the lake and drive into the town. One

long road effectively the centre, busy with traffic, tractors and buses, lined with pubs and caffs and a Spar and a post office and various but not varying souvenir stores offering postcards and snapshot books and dolls in shawls and stovepipe hats and crockery and other similar ware. More fudge, and chutney and marmalade. And the telegraph wires spanning this busy road draped with banners bilingual advertising the coming eisteddfod.

—Can yeh see a chipper anywhere, Ally? Pure fuckin starvin, I am. Fancy some jockeys. Can't see one anywhere.

—There's one, over the road.

—Where?

Alastair points.

—How djer know that's a chipper? Looks more like a caff just, to me.

—Cos it says, look: pysgod a sglodion. That means fish an chips. I remember from visitin me nan, like.

—Mad fuckin language. An youse can fuck off n all, yeh pairer Taff cunts.

Darren squeezes the car into a space ahead of a rusting pick-up poised to reverse into it. The passenger's head appears out the window, flat cap and creased complexion red as if boiled, sees whatever he sees in Darren's expectant leer and mutters something to the driver and the pick-up pulls away.

Darren grins. —Sheepshaggin cunts, fuck off. What yis avin, Ally? Just chips, yeh?

—Yeh. An a coupla rolls if thee've got any. An a can of lemmo or somethin, Coke.

—Alright. Darren cranes his head to look out

through the windscreen. —Where is it again? I've lost the fuckin thing.

Alastair points. —Just there, look.

—I can't see it. What's it called?

—Ddraig Goch. It means –

—Oh yeh, I've gorrit. An I don't give two fucks what it means so sod off an shurrup.

Darren leaves the car, slams the door, waits for a gap in the traffic then crosses the road at a jog. Alastair watches him go.

And dragon red dragon close enough to smell your leathern wings. Near enough now under you to feel the shade from your spread pinions, the shockwave of chilled air rocking me as they beat. Both your being and your myth accessible on these outer peaks if they could be reached and the evasive lake beast and the rumbling black clouds overhead and the coiled viper, the springing serpent, your being and the myth inside that being and the hot memory inside that all also coiled like your scaled tail in a child's nocturnal imaginings. Your fiery breath detectable alone in adult anger.

Alastair observes Darren enter the chipper then slides the fudge box off his knees into the well at his feet and stretches and yawns. Joints snap, crack like matchsticks. He examines his fingernails then regards the speedometer and seems fixated on that dial for some moments then he grunts and shakes his head as if ridding it of some unpleasant thought and removes his cap and runs a palm over his shaven skull, likes the feel and the sound of the stubble rasping on his spread hand. The lump like a ball-bearing beneath the thin skin where a policeman's boot chipped bone. He enjoys this proof that his skull is bare, odd phrenologist self-assessing his cranial topography, scally quack self-diagnostic. He replaces the cap on his head and tugs the peak low then whistles tunelessly then spreads his legs and pulls the crotch of his kex away from his skin, freeing the sweat trapped there between flesh and trackie. Such a sustained sitting position and the gathering dampness uncomfortable. Small sigh of relief. Small brown crust on his knee which he picks and scrapes at, a salt pan in miniature, some spilled gravy or sauce now dried to a crust and cracked brown and scaly like the bed of Bala Lake should it ever be drained which maybe it should since it is the only way to be sure about the monster. But even then some secret underwater tunnel to another lake, an underground lake unknown to men. Alastair scrapes this stain away with a fingernail then lights and quickly smokes a cigarette, staring through glass at moving people, thin streams of grey smoke from his nostrils huffed against the glass to break soft then drift and disperse across. Turns slightly sideways to drop the butt out of the open window.

A passing figure stops. This figure too in baseball hat and tracksuit, trainies and a dragon T-shirt underneath the open jacket whereas Alastair wears a Carlsberg one and Alastair looks up into this figure's face, into the eyes shaded by the hat peak but slit still and dark and the crannied face beneath them tight lips and this face studies his in turn and without smiling they nod at each other, one small quick forward thrust of the neck more like an abbreviated headbutt than any gesture of acquaintance and in that one terse nod mirrored there is a recognition, immediate and profound, a tacit acknowledgement of some shared thing, deeper in them than bone. A suggestion perhaps that each understands the other's existence and accepts utterly the unfathomable attributes of that, of them.

The figure walks away. Hisses watery spittle through his teeth and turns into a pub. Alastair refaces front, zips his jacket up to his chin. A hot plastic bag is dumped on to his knees through the wound-down window.

—Eeyar, lad. Grab old of tha.

Darren gets back into the car. —Alright?

—Sound, yeh.

—Go down by the lake, yeh? Av ar dinner down by the lake, like. Might even see that fuckin monster of yours, eh?

Darren starts the engine and pulls out into the traffic.

—Whatjer get me?

—Chips. That's all yeh asked for, innit?

—No rolls?

—Didn't av any. Sold out thee said.

—Aw. Just fancied a chip butty.

—Stop whingein. I got yer a can of shandy, what more djer friggin want?

They retrace their route through the small low town and park up at the near end of the lake in the designated spaces there. As dark as molten lead the lake and flattened to the far horizon, flanked by mountains and some dark tree tufts and white dots of cottages on those mountains, even smaller white dots of grazing sheep. Some boats bob on the lake; some windsurfers tread water and hold on to their boards, waiting for the air to move. Noiseless but for the grumbles and guffaws of ducks and the rhythmic splat of the lake's little waves.

The car fills up with smell, snared vinegar air. Chewing at food and slurping at cans, no talk. Darren wolfs his, chucks the paper out of the window, restarts the car with gleaming hands.

—What yeh doin?

—We've gorrer nash, lar. Can't wait for you to finish yer dinner.

—But there's loads left.

—Hard fuckin luck. Eat em on the move, well.

Alastair crams another handful into his mouth, balls the paper and the remaining bits up and as they turn parallel to the lake he throws the package out of the window into the shallows. It unfurls on the surface and chips spill, sink like little yellow submarines. Ducks scurry.

—Feedin the fish, ey, feller? Good lad.

Darren veers the vehicle away from the water. The gwyniad slowly rising from the lakebed silt, shrugging age-thick slime off its fins and scales and turning, swinging in its complete uniqueness towards this new food. Sole fish with sole station on this earth rising and gulping moon-eyed from blackness to rippling shadow to light green haze to –

Darren punches Alastair on the leg.

—Ow!

—Come ed, Ally. Stay focused, lar. You've gorrer read the map for us.

Alastair reaches down for the road atlas. And an old perch battle-scarred, a crescent bite in its dorsal fin and one eye milky recognising the new smell in the lake, a memory unfolding of that same smell on small human hands so many years ago and those hands clasping it and squeezing it and trapping it in a bright and gasping world, a world panting and a world blinding and this old perch capo now of this black lake turning away from that smell and the memory creeping like the grease through the icy water.

—Alastair.

And some huge beast whale-sized and long-snouted powering through the darkness–

—ALASTAIR!

—What?

—Wake up, yeh cunt! Switch yerself on, yeh fuckin divvy! Where the fuck do I go now?

Alastair points to a road sign and opens the atlas on his knees. Glances back over his shoulder, once, sees the balled chip paper, some small buoy grease-streaked, and above the shrinking lake a cloud as wide as that lake and as dark fails to burst and begins to drift south.

The sign reads:

ABERYSTWYTH

62

SHORE

Dinnertime. It's the time of day for food, the designated hour to eat. Plus I'm bloody starvin.

I go into Y Popty an buy two sausage rolls, a chilli pasty, two bread rolls for the birds an a styrofoam cup of coffee. The girl puts all this stuff on the glass counter top an hands me a placcy bag. I smile at her an spread me arms to show her – the whole one an the half a one in the empty sleeve. Thee unbalance, like.

—Oh. Sorry, bach.

—That's alright.

She puts the stuff in the bag for me an hands it over the counter an I take it then have to put it down on the floor while I dig in me pocket for money and give the money to her an take the change off her an put it back in me pocket an say thanks then bend an pick up the bag by the handles. Leave the shop an turn right, down towards the beach. Me belly rumblin; loud, like a lorry passin yer bedroom window in the middle of the night. I'm hungry.

Christ, try buyin yer dinner with only one fuckin arm. Try carryin it down on to the beach. Try fuckin *eatin* it.

Packed, town is. All the people on their lunch breaks like, an students shoppin or driftin or doin wharrever the fuck it is that students generally do. When they're not standin at cashpoint machines talkin far too loudly about film, that is. Or brayin like fuckin donkeys in the pubs. A *Big Issue* seller outside W.H. Smith's is shoutin out the name of his mag an a couple of doors down, in the doorway of a derelict shop that used to be another bakery, sits the rugby-shirted hulk of Ikey Pritchard. Even from over the road I can kind of sense his presence, the solidity of him, the volume of air he displaces. Just got out of nick apparently but that hasn't diminished him any; he was inside for beatin one of his mates to death or somethin, but that mate was apparently a killer himself, something like that – sordid and horrible, wharrever the fuck it was. He's leanin forward, elbows on his knees, readin a newspaper folded several times into a small, thick square. He glances up at me as I pass then glances back down again, no nod. Probly doesn't recognise me or remember me cos it's been a while since I saw him last an spoke to him at the fair, just before he got locked up. Or he could just be a rude twat, couldn't he? Not that I'd ever tell him, like; don't wanner lose me *other* arm as well. Ikey fuckin balloonhead. Nutter hillbilly bastard.

The promenade stinks of rotten seaweed. That foul, salty, dead-fish stink. Almost alien to any familiar human sense, you can taste it an smell it at the same time, almost see an hear it as well, a shimmering haze like heat and a hum like bees – it's like we need another sense to assimilate the things in the sea, when thee interact with ar lives, like. They're disturbing to us, sort of unnerving. Maybe that's why the prom's so empty now, like, cos of the pong from the beached seaweed. It's keepin people away. Bet the castle grounds're chocka with all the people on their dinner hour, triner find somewhere to chill away from the niffy promenade. Sea'll take it back soon enough. Waves'll turn around an reclaim it.

—Oi! D'ya wanna boi a second-hand car? D'ya wanna boi a second-hand car?!

One of the Aber halfwits, the wetbrains like, sittin on a bench by Phinikki's burger bar an shoutin nonsense into space. So many of them in this small town, a disproportionate amount really, shouters an screamers, street drinkers. This particular one has been here years, longer than I have, and his mind has disintegrated publicly; he used to go on in pubs about bein a writer, then he started sharin the bevvy with the crusties on the prom, an before yeh could say 'Stop it now, Christ, save yerself' he became what he's been since – a permanent fixture on the prom in his filthy clothes shoutin this disconnected, nonsensical, stream-of-dying-consciousness garbage. Sad really.

An ahl woman walks past him with a shoppin trolley.

—D'ya wanna boi a second-hand car? IT RUNS ON SCHIZOPHRENIA!

She scurries away head down an he cackles an coughs. Sad, really. But, then again, he's always been a bit of a cunt. Eighteen cans of Spesh a day has really only turned him into a *louder* cunt.

I go down on to the beach, sit with me back against the sea wall, lookin out at thee ocean. The smell down here don't bother me, nor does the shouting knob-jockey behind me; I can just shut it all out easy enough. Only disconnect. Retreat into yourself an what yeh know, what you've learned, all the stuff that keeps yeh rooted, keeps yeh sane –

– that there are over two million people in Britain with a chronic addiction to drink an drugs. That's one fuck of a lot of people, an each one of them finds being in their own minds a horribly uncomfortable place to be. They do not welcome themselves. They'd sooner have the sick, the shits, the carnage, the dissolving consciousness. The trembling, God, the trembling; me first night in detox, I got covered in fuckin soup, an not just me own, either. Imagine Jerry Lee Lewis, Shakin Stevens, a pack of shitting dogs with distemper in the same room, during an earth tremor – *that's* how much tremblin was goin on. It was ridiculous. And always the questions, the incessant probing, Peter Salt swooping like a hawk, the deep V of wrinkles between his faded grey eyes pronounced and his never-ending fuckin questions. Thee interrogation.

I bite into a sausage roll. The wind whips me collar up against me cheek. The sea's mood is changing, darkening, it seems.

Some of the things Peter Salt told me:

The drink makes you make the choices you make. You are powerless. You are nothing but an alky.

Your problem is not drink and drugs, your problem is not being able to cope with your feelings.

My job is to get people through this tiny little doorway called 'recovery'.

Addicts can be the most intelligent people going through their lives doing increasingly stupid things.

You are

you are

you're

Good sausage rolls from Y Popty. Peppery, kind of. I wolf one an start on thee other. Should a bought three. I bolt the second as well an then break up the bread rolls for the birds; this involves holding the roll in me mouth an peckin bits off it with me hand, like thee opposite of feeding, like an anti-dinner. I gather the bits in me hand an scatter them across the pebbles, as far away from me as I can, an open me coffee an sip it an eat me chilli pasty an watch the birds, the gulls an the crows an the pigeons, descend squabblin on the bread. I like to watch em as thee land, spreadin their wings; silhouetted against the weak sun, it's like light is spillin from their wings. Like light throbs in their feathers.

The shouting behind me gets fainter as thee alky staggers off along the prom, down towards Constitution Hill. That was me, once – down thee Albert Dock or Otterspool prom, staggerin, swayin, reeling, having a conversation with ghosts, Christ, the Grim fuckin Reaper. Me clothes a crust of old leakages or a pond of new ones an that was where it got me, the quest for joy – to booze to Rebecca to insanity to the severing an cremation of one of me limbs. Voices mutterin out of the taps, out of plugholes, drains. In kettles, in pillar boxes on the street. Muttering about me. Talking about me. And the stench seeping with the pus from the rot in me arm an still putting a needle in that rot an still drinking past the burst veins in me throat. Ever-present taste of blood. Still pouring poison on me ulcers an inner sores an the blood feathery in the bog water and like blackcurrant jam in me underwear.

Because I was bored. Because I could see nothing of any attraction outside of Rebecca an the holy choir in me head when I was drunk or otherwise wrecked.

Because, I'll say it again, I was BORED fuckin BORED.

Because there was nobody else like me in the world because I drank because I was divinely afflicted because I was chosen because I was too good for this fuckin world because without the drink I could not bear to live an because my life now is only half a life compared to when I was most drunken the thumping blood the yearning heart the closest to satisfaction ever the the the the the

pitiful fucking wretch

Bright red legs among the yellow of the gulls' and the black of the crows' at the scattered bread. Smaller than the gulls this bird

flew like fucking I did

soared like I did like

I fuckin could when I when I

when I was

Common tern, widespread summer visitor, essentially pale grey above an white below but underparts on occasion have pale greyish wash. Red legs and black cap and orange-red bill black-tipped, this is adult summer plumage and colouring and bill can be pure red or almost even entirely black. Tail deeply forked. Flight: hovers aerial dive strong and powerful swims and air-dives perches on and can take off and land from both water and ground frequents sea and estuaries and inland freshwater. Food: fish. And of course broken bits of bread bestowed by a one-armed ex-jakey. Breeds along most coasts in concentrated colonies of one to one thousand and also in smaller numbers inland the common tern do not confuse with other terns most notably Arctic or Roseate.

Not particularly common, the common tern. I watch him snatch up a big piece of bread an flap away to eat it at the waterline which is becoming more ragged now as the wind picks up. I finish me coffee and put all the empty bags n stuff back into the placcy bag an zip me fleece right up to me neck an light a ciggie. Me stump begins to burn as the temperature drops.

A one-legged pigeon is tryin to get himself some bread. Mucky little bugger, town pigeon, one leg completely rotted off. I'm willing him to get a bit of roll but thee other birds all beat him to it but then he does get a piece an tries to hop away with it but a big gull stabs his back until he drops it an the gull gulps it an the stumpy pidge resumes his pointless pecking. Poor wee fucker. Ends up just kind of circling the feeding birds, circling an cooing an pecking at pebbles. Stumblin on his one good leg, his one *only* leg.

And all the missing limbs of the world stacked up in one sky-high pyramid, the size an volume of a mountain. All the previous owners stumblin around abbreviated, unwhole; Tutsi women in headscarves, no hands; children playin in minefields in Burma, Afghanistan, Cambodia, the Congo, Foday Sankoh's limbless little orphans. These thousands of shortened people, this hobbling horde of amputees. Moving around part dead on the planet, legs gone, arms gone, incomplete. This worldwide truncation. This global reduction of the human shape.

Yeh, well. There is a shape that can't be drawn, can't be traced, cannot be hacked. So fuck youse.

So that's it, that's dinner. I bury me cigarette filter in the sand an stand an put the plastic bag of rubbish in a bin an leave the beach an the birds an head towards the supermarket, through town. There's shoppin to be done. I'm movin quickly cos a great big black cloud has drifted above the town down from the north an I don't wanner be caught under it when it bursts.

Step 5: We admitted to God, to ourselves an to another human being the exact nature of ar wrongs. Which was exactly a hubristic one which if we had've been given the possibility of achieving bliss or even the mental apparatus to comprehend what it even is would not've been a part of ar make-up in the first fucking place an thus we would've had no need to seek it through drink or drugs as a means of expanding the stunted human template. But admit it we did an God gave absolutely no sign of acknowledgement, no flame flickering in ar darknesses an I already knew it anyway which was why I yearned for the bottle and Peter Salt said I was both acting an denying my essential self which was to be secretive and shy. So that I was still duplicitous, still behaving in an obsessive alky fashion so I went away to think about it an Peter Salt said I was isolating an self-pitying. So welcome back to sobriety; this ludicrous place of judgement an confusion. This spiritless plain of order an boredom an denial an flatness an negative reward NEGA-TIVE REWARD NEGATIVE REWARD this life.

CAR

—God, it's gunner rain, Da. Look at that cloud. Completely fuckin black.

Another approaching Morris Minor flashes its lights. An old couple in this car, he with a flat cap and tweed jacket and driving gloves and she with pink-tinted spectacles and a headscarf, both of them together like a visitation from the past or dimension-drifters from a place parallel of day trips and cosiness. Darren presses the V fingers against his side window as they pass.

—Another fuckin flashin cunt. The fuck's wrong with these blerts?

Alastair points. —Look at the fog, Da. We're gunner drive right into it.

Darren squints. —That's not fog, softlad. It's fuckin smoke.

—Is it?

—Yeh.

—What from?

—I don't fuckin know, do I? Somethin burnin in the field. Some poor fucker's holiday home or somethin. Some mad fuckin Welshies burnin some poor ahl cunt's retirement home that he's worked hard all his fuckin life to afford. Probly in the friggin war an everythin. Twats, thee are.

And if this dark approaching miasma is cloud black-

bellied with rain it hangs too low and does not drift
and if it is fog it is too dark and oily and it appears
to rise from the ground with some odd quality of heft
and grease. And the car crests a small hill and from
that vantage point they can see the fire creating this
clotted cloud the flames crimson not orange or yellow
but the bright red of a wound and in those flames
shapes stiff and blackened and tangled in posture
suggestive of pain as if Satan himself stirs. As if this
green and rising earth has rent to reveal such secret
fever as seethes never-ending beneath, the flames and
the torment on which we move and build our homes
and play our games. And what such aspirations reach
towards and only result in such hot devouring.

—The fuck is that, Ally?

—It's, aw, Jesus fuckin Christ. I've seen these on the
telly.

—The fuck is it, lar?

Tongues, tendrils of sticky smoke busy with motes
ash grey and pink-frilled, lap at the windscreen. Splots
of wet ash adhere, shunted by the wipers, leaving trails
of streaky grease.

—It's the fuckin, it's that fuckin foot n mouth
thingio. Thee must be burnin all the dead animals.

—Is that wharrit is? All the dead cows, like?

—Yeh.

—Should a brought some rolls an some brown sauce.
Could've had a crackin friggin barbie, lar, eh?

But Darren does not smile. They drive slow through
a cloud of smuts and soots and fume reeking burnt
from hide and horn and flesh and bone and they pull
parallel to the pyre itself and can now discern the

scorched shapes, the thin sticks of curved rib or hoofed leg trapped and blackened in these adoptions of agony within the red hysterical thrashing of the flames. Horned skulls bellow fire and ribcages clasp nothing but darting scarlet organs. And nothing of any life about this huge beast-burning, this unattended charnel churning at basin-bottom formed by this ring of mountains which appear through the fumes to lean eagerly into this atrocious furnace, to bow in abeyance or poise to pounce on the smoking dregs, just charred chips of bone and horn steaming in boiled-blood slurry. Fat-marbled offerings to these vast surrounding scavengers. Abhorrent ponded pudding to appease the greedy soil.

Consciously or not, Darren decelerates and they chug past the pyre, the mass cremation, all four eyes turned left towards the fire. This scene from fever or nightmare or concocted from the seared hemispheres of drugs or drink. Crackling apparition, spitting vision hewn in the steam from adrenalin-overloaded lobes.

—Jesus fuckin Christ.

Alastair says nothing, just stares. His head craning back over his shoulder as if joined to that burning, as if snagged by a tentacle of damp smoke.

—The fuckin *stink*, Jesus.

Like nothing imaginable, like the earth's bowels burst and all the shit of its history, the past and ongoing splat and clamour of its life. The reeking ashy end of all endeavour. Hearts popping in great heat like puff-balls and releasing nothing but dust.

—Gorrer friggin gerrout of here, lar. Tellin yeh. Not fuckin right, this place. Somethin just not fuckin right abahr it. Feel fuckin *sick*, Jesus.

Darren accelerates as fast as the elderly engine will allow. Claws of smoke are yanked away from the car by the sudden wind drag and they leave the clutch of the dark cloud, re-enter cleaner air.

—Fuckin freaked me *right* out, that has. Tellin yeh. Really fuckin freaked me out. Sooner we're back over the border the fuckin better, I shit yis not. Fuckin Tommy. Not worth *this* fuckin shit, no fuckin way. Next time he needs summin sorted in *this* bleedin shithole he can do it his own fuckin self, tellin yeh. Jesus fuckin Christ. The fuck's goin on here, Ally, ey? Like the fuckin dark ages or summin, a big fuckin war or summin. It's fuckin mad. An look at *that.*

He shows Alastair the back of his left hand, the cleg-fly bite there now hardened into a berry-sized maroon lump.

—See that? Cunt *still* fuckin hurts. An why've *you* gone so quiet all of a fuckin sudden?

Alastair shrugs. —Not much to say, like, is there? Am just thinkin, that's all.

—Wharrabout? Ah no, don't tell me. Am fuckin freaked out enough as it is. Get this fuckin stupid cunt of a job done an get back to the 'Pool, that's all I wanner do. Stupid fuckin . . . Can of ale an a line of beak back in me own gaff, that's what I want. None a *this* fuckin shite. Tempted to sack the whole friggin thing off. Just crack on to Tommy we couldn't find the cunt, like.

Alastair turns his head to face him. —Honest? Yeh serious?

Darren shrugs and snorts.

—But a mean what if we can't find im anyway, for

real, like? This one-armed feller? Might not be able to find im anyway.

—So what?

—Well, T would never know, would he? Never know that we, erm, turned back, like. I mean, we could do it. If yeh wanted to. *I* wouldn't say anythin.

Darren snorts again. —No, cos it'd be the last ever fuckin thing yer'd say, that's why.

He falls silent for a moment then says: —Nah, listen, someone's gunner pay for this friggin shite. *Some* fucker's gorrer take the whack, like, so it might as well be this one-armed cunt. Or that other musher, that Downey. I mean, at least that way we'll be gettin paid for it, knowmean?

A large dead tree approaches. Through the warped limbs of this tree some sooty streamers of slimy smoke still swirl like bad bunting put out for the homecoming of some demon and beneath this tree so adorned at its bulging muscular roots a group of crows some twenty in number cavort; they hop excitedly on the spot on the ground then as one they hurl themselves up into the wind, flap cackling against it for several beats then drift down groundwards again. Hop, launch, descend. Only ever chest-high off the earth their black wings spread-fingered and inky in the wind their beaks agape as if in some form of laughter. Facing the beast-burning and launching themselves, hop and rise and flap almost victorious, celebratory.

—Look at all them black birds, Darren. Why're thee doin that?

—Doin what?

—Jumpin up in thee air like that. Look, thee keep

doin it. Why do thee keep on flappin up n down like tha?

—Fucked if I know, Ally. The fuck djer think I am, Bill fuckin Oddie?

They draw level with and then pass the birds and Alastair swivels his head on the pivot of his neck to watch them and their leaping. —I wonder why thee do that, he says softly and not entirely without awe, shifting in his seat so as to longer regard the leaping black birds, their ragged tribe, the mystery of their movements beneath the dead and leafless tree and the ink-plumed enigma of their gathering.

Another road sign:

ABERYSTWYTH

50

SUPERMARKET 1

I love all these bright colours, love just standin here among all the bright, clean colours of the fruit an vegetables an the smell comin off them, the melons an lemons an onions. It's so nice, clean. Even the wee clods of mud on the spuds, it seems clean an fresh an kind of appetising; the dark soil an these things comin out of it, boil em up with butter. Dead nice. An the leeks so white with their wee wormy roots an the deep green of their tough top leaves, they'd make a squeakin noise if yeh bit into em. But I imagine holdin one to me nose an breathin in the scent of it, that sharp an oniony whiff. God, me belly's rumblin; just had me dinner but these leeks're makin me belly rumble. An I don't feel hungry, either; wonder if it's possible for yer belly to grumble with a hunger for somethin other than food?

Not that I need to buy much here, in the fruit n veg aisle. Most of the veggies on display here I grow meself, in me back garden: cabbages an radishes an carrots an parsnips an potatoes. Tried lettuces one time but the fuckin slugs massacred em. Et em all to shreds in one night, thee entire friggin row. Slimy little bastards. But thee other stuff, the root crops like, I grow them, I make them appear from the muck; I plant the wee seeds an nurture them, water them an feed them an mix me compost heap an scatter it over them tiny, tiny seeds no bigger than yer little finger-nail an wait for the first green shoots to poke through an then coax from the soil, from them tiny, tiny seeds, somethin as big an bright as a carrot, say, or a parsnip. It's fuckin amazin how such things can come from such wee seeds, innit? An from the dirt as well an from my care an attention. Don't need two arms to do it, either, one's plenty – yeh only need the one arm to make food from nowt. Or almost nowt. I fuckin love it, I do; here is my patch of thee earth an from it I will form my food. A patch of muck all barren an useless but I will tend it an nurse it an make it invaluable. All that stuff goin on under the soil as I sleep, the seeds splitting, developing, reachin upwards towards the light an the tubers bulgin an blooming with all the goodness an it's only me who makes that, only me. Makes all that lovely stuff come from the dirty ground. It's ace; Alan friggin Titchmarsh, that's me. Except without bein quite such an irritatin knob, obviously.

Shoppin with one arm is a pain in thee arse, tho; can't just reach an grab an drop things in a basket, no, you've gorrer put the basket down on the deck, take whatever it is yeh want off the shelf, put it in the basket an then pick the basket up again an move along to the next item yeh want an do the same friggin thing all over again, all over again n again, endlessly. All that friggin stoopin, stoppin n startin, drives yeh fuckin mental. But no other way round it, is there? Unless yeh practise usin one of yer feet as a hand like chimps do.

Prehensile, that's the word. Prehensile.

Celery. Charlie loves celery. Personally, I can't stand the stringy green shite but me rabbit's fuckin well up for it, loves a stick of celery, he does. He can't stand carrots, tho; put one of *them* in his hutch an two weeks later you'll take it back out again, unnibbled, black an soft an rotten. Thought *all* rabbits love carrots; that's like a mouse not likin cheese. So Charlie eats the celery an I eat the carrots. I grow carrots, but I don't grow celery; I buy that. Too much friggin hassle growin celery for a rabbit, responsibility or not. Only costs fifty pee a bunch anyway.

I put the basket on the floor, drop a packet of celery into it. Leave it there as I get meself some loose onions. Now *this* is fucking awkward; I snatch a bag off the roll, one of them thin Cellophane bags, open it with me teeth an fingers an then rest it, open, on the swedes underneath thee onions an drop five, six onions into it. Then I grab one of the handles on the wee bag an pull it up so that it straightens an thee onions tumble into it, at least that's thee idea, but it's friggin lopsided an it collapses an thee onions spill an roll across the swedes an fall to the floor ah fuck it.

—Don't worry, I'll get them.

—Thanks.

—Not a problem.

Young woman at me feet, pickin up thee onions. Straight brown hair an a lovely face.

—I'll get you some more cos these'll be all bruised now.

She replaces the fallen onions an starts putting new ones into the bag.

—How many d'you want?

—About six please.

—No bother.

She bags six onions then knots the handles of the bag together. I watch her two hands working, twisting quickly against each other, the faint veins beneath her skin an the tendons working. Fuckin amazing machine. So many moving parts, so intricate, so perfect.

Christ. How long is it since I had a shag?

—Here you go.

—Ta very much.

—No problem at all.

She smiles at me then turns an takes up her own basket an walks away down thee aisle to the fresh-fish chiller. Ace, kind, friendly young woman. There are angels fuckin everywhere, aren't there? Not many of them I'd like to have sex with, tho.

How long. How long. Pathetic fucker can't even bag onions properly need help need someone else how long is it since skin smell, since another hand on yer dick that smell eyes so close to another face so long so long useless fucker need help to shop. Useless ex-alky stain on the planet.

Fuck off. Fuck *off*.

I put the bag of onions in me basket an pick me basket up again. Beetroot in the basket, cucumber in the basket, lettuce iceberg. Turn to the fresh fruit an there are

oh lemons

yellow lemons

bright yellow dimpled lemons with a nipple at each end and

Rebecca slicing lemons her movements temazepam-slow as if under water the knife slowly slicing through the pitted yellow peel the pith like a layer of subcutaneous fat an then the marbled segments triangular in cross-section made up of many thousands of tiny teardrops an the pips in them like artefacts precious things buried in ice

Becca's hair hanging

her lower lip drooping temazepam-slow

tem azzzzzz ep ammm slooooooooooowww

delicate thin fingers peeling the slices off the chopping board an the wet rings thee left on the scored wood an then raising slowly placing slowly the lemon slices in the glass of gin an then thee angered fizzing an the clicking of thee ice

money from somewhere cos we had gin

money from somewhere cos we had fuckin lemons

an what unknowable was in that gin, what big gin mystery was in that glass: where would we be when we'd drunk the bottle I did not know I could not know an that was the pull, that was the draw the magnetic fuckin attraction the surrender

the bubbles bursting in me nostrils as I gulped that alcohol so clear so sharp slicing through the furry mould in me gob an the fog in me head an the whole world and its history pourin into me opening skull me mind so open so welcoming so pure fuckin alive

—Can yew excuse me there please?

SNAP and an old lady is edging in front of me starin at me strangely. I must've been standin here gawkin at the lemons for how long? How long? Too long to be conventionally acceptable anyway, so I apologise an move away an the woman watches me go as she bags up some lemons. Probly for her drinks tonight as she sits at her window with her husband an watches the sun sink into the sea an they're sippin at gin an tonics or vodkas with lemonade or cola or grapefruit or cranberry or anythin as long as it's mixed with the fuckin VODKA

this taste

fuck it

Stoop, basket down, stand, pick, stoop, basket up. Apples in the basket, some tangerines in the basket, both pre-bagged, the tangers in one of them wee orange netty things like odd, round, orange fish. And talkin of fish; I move over to the seafood fridge, put the basket down, take up a mackerel an some salmon fishcakes, drop them in the basket an pick the basket up again. Gettin heavier. Walk over to the deli counter an do the same. Fucking. Thing with half a pound of farmhouse Cheddar.

It can drive yeh fucking crazy, this. Drive yeh right out of yer fuckin head. All this stuff, it's relentlessly there, always in yer life this stooping an pickin an bendin, so much time spent doin this shit an the reason why it drives yeh mad is because yer instinct is to fight it; yer instinct is to reach out with thee arm that isn't there to facilitate these insistent necessities, these nagging fuckin necessities. And all that happens is yer empty sleeve flaps an you can almost feel yer fingers closing, almost feel the cold stoniness of the melon, say, in yer non-existent palm, but it's not fuckin there. Only in yer head is it there still or in some other place where consciousness resides an it's pointless an it's embarrassing an it can threaten to drive you away from yer own fuckin mind because

becausebecausebecausebecausebecaaaaaauuuuuusse

because you fight it. Because yeh can't let the memories go. Cos you always want things to be better, always, to be improved an it perpetually seems that suffering to you, loss to you, is not an essential part of your being, it is some alien thing imposed from without thrust like a knife into your life an your life should be easy your life should weigh little an beneath all that the background to that assumption is that you were born in blood, you were born in screams an anguish an so whatever comes after that vast upheaval may only wash over you like rain.

Like the, like the, the cowering rabbit with the hawk swooping or the fox coming out of the shadows oh I don't fucking know I know this I need some rice.

Easycook rice in the basket, spaghetti in the basket. Tins: baked beans plum tomatoes soup peas both mushy an garden. Green mushy garden made soft by storm.

I pass my Onion Girl by the bread racks an smile at her an she smiles back. She's got a big pizza in her basket, I notice, stickin up like a sail; ham an pineapple. Yick. Never been one for that sweet/savoury mix, me, never gone for that at all. Ham an pineapple? What's that all about? Where the fuck did *that* combination come from? I mean, yeh wouldn't mix cherries with fishfingers, now, would yeh? Would yeh?

I stop by the newspaper/magazine rack to pick up a *Cambrian News*. Glossy, light-reflectin covers of all them magazines, everythin on offer here that is not food or love yet promotes itself as both. Every gesture false towards improvability in this flat an shining form an it is all so flimsy, such feeble fumblin towards an unattainable end. So quick to crumble, betrayal in its atoms. Beckham's fucking face on several covers; what's he got now, what newsworthy thing, some new fuckin tattoo? Ooh, must read about that. Must read what he's got to say about his wedding to his fame-rapacious permatanned human stick insect of a wife. Purple thrones, fuck off. A ten-foot by ten-foot blow-up of their faces kissing, fuck off. Distraction distraction must have this distraction, ANYTHING to stop me thinking to divert my mind from the terror of absence, from the gulf at the core of my being. Beckham Williams Halliwell, come distract me, *save* me, tug me into the soulless mediocrity that is the world we've made for arselves. It's safe for me in that world. In that world, pain can be banished with a smirk an a camera flash.

Aw, just fuck off.

Yet whether the value if any value there may be is in such futility an the forms we give yearning nevertheless such tatty attire still must mean

Fuck off.

Don't ask me. I've got shoppin to do. Pick up the local paper an it's in me hand yet I don't *feel* it in me hand, don't feel the paper against me skin. Happens sometimes, this; peripheral necritis, it's called – a wasting disease of the nerve ends in which all tactile sensation is booze-blasted away in thee extremities. See thee alkies with the burnt n blistered fingers where cigarettes have burnt down an cooked the skin without them noticing. See the nails bitten bloody during DTs. See the see the see the

Paper in the basket, glossy mag in there too. Don't know or care which one, just that it's got Jennifer Lopez on the cover. Crap singer, crap actress, but . . . flippin eck. She's wearin a bikini. Thee arse on her.

How long's it been? Too fuckin long.

Stoop again, pick up again. Gettin a wee bit heavy now. A short-haired girl who I recognise vaguely is usin me as a screen as she slips a frozen steak inside her coat so I stand there til she's finished an she grins an pats me on the back an I smile in reply an move on, past the dairy counter, the damaged-goods stand where I used to shop, an into thee alcohol aisle, which hums.

Step 6: We were entirely ready to have God remove all these defects of character. Yeh, cos we were completely incapable of doing so arselves cos we abjured every semblance of responsibility cos we were just alkies, we were just drunks. An as if God cared anyway, as if He repented of the broken way He made us or even of the ways He broke us, as if pity and compassion were for some reason now going to prompt even a blink in His empty yellow eyes when they never had before. Our prayer: Remove these defects of character. Scorch away from us the fallibilities we recognise and hold to us keenly cos they overpower us, they devour the weak nestlings that we are, so we must make as if there is nothing of us to take, so strip ar skin, remove ar limbs, build from us just bones. Amen.

CAR

The village they drive through appears deserted. A shop boarded up, flat planks for windows and a shut pub perhaps permanently that way and some grey stone cottages no smoke from their chimneys and gardens overgrown and dirty grey nets behind windows like a film on lifeless eyes. Over the graveyard wall, long tangled creepers spill as if behind that wall a giant crustie lies supine, his dreads flung over the mossed stones he uses as a pillow. As if the Titan Idris himself unwashed and unbarbered rests flat among the slate stones, with their legends, arranged upright around him. And one skinny cat at these graveyard gates, small and tatty tabby sentinel, simply blinks green eyes once and slowly as the old car trundles past.

—Fuckin ell, Ally. All's this place needs is a friggin tumbleweed, innit?

—Is right.

—It's dead. Friggin ghost town, lar.

—Ghost village.

—Yeh.

They pass a school and on the wall surrounding the playground is some graffiti in white block capitals as if to the writer neatness had the same import as message.

NID YW CYMRU
AR WERTH

RHYDDID!

DAL DY DIR

NA I'R MEWNLIFIAD

Darren points.

—What's that mean?

—How'm *I* supposed to know?

—Well, you speak this mad fuckin language, don't yeh?

—Just know a few words, that's all. Don't exactly friggin *speak* it or anythin. Just picked up a few words from me nan.

—Still know more than I do.

—Yeh, but I don't know what *that* means.

—What?

—*That.* Alastair gestures to the past with a backwards jerk of his head. —Them words on the wall.

—Just thought yeh might, that's all.

—Well, I don't.

—Alright, well, fine; yeh don't. What's the fuckin cob on for?

—Not cobby. Just tired, like. Fuckin fed up.

—Is right. Shoulda brought some fuckin beak. Took the risk with the bizzies, like.

They leave the village and enter a wood. A pine wood, therefore new but still old enough for shadows to have sprouted at root and between the ranked trunks. Old enough for the trees to be entwined at branch, for them to appear close-packed and supportive and secretive. To be barrier-like.

—Bit creepy, this, Da.

—Whole fuckin country's creepy, lad. Saw the fuckin thing off an lerrit float away.

Alastair watches the long shadows scoot across the bonnet. Thin dark shadows like liquid.

The car lurches across the road. One sudden violent lurch.

—JESUS CHRIST, DARREN! FUCK'S SAKE!

Impact with barrier narrowly avoided and the engine screams as Darren calmly straightens the car. Big grin.

—The fuckin hell are yeh playin at?

—I was triner see wharrit'd be like to drive with only one arm. Changin gear an stuff.

—Fuckin suicidal's wharrit'd be like, Christ. Near fuckin shit meself then I did. Jesus.

—Djer think he drives, this stumpy cunt? I mean, if yeh lose an arm, yeah, can yeh get some kind of special car? Steerin's easy like, burrit's the gear changes that're a pisser. Even an automatic'd be a pain in thee arse.

—Maybe there's some kind of special thingio. Change gear with yer foot or somethin.

—Yer *foot*?

—Yeh, y'know. Never seen them disabled cars? Must be some way round it, I suppose. Or maybe just one gear, like.

—Then yer'd be dead slow.

—Still quicker than walkin, tho, innit?

—Suppose, yeh. Be a bit friggin biffy, tho.

—Safer than *you* still, yeh twat.

Darren grins. —Ah, stop yer whinin. Gave yer a bit of excitement, didn't it?

—Could've lost me *own* friggin arm then.

—Oh aye? How?

—In the crash, like. Imagine that, ey, goin back to Tommy an we've both lost ar arms as well. Be dead funny that, wouldn't it?

—Losin me arm? No.

—No, I mean . . .

—If yer *had* to lose a limb, like, I mean if somebody said yer could lose a limb or be wasted, like, what would it be? An arm or a leg?

—Me arm, deffo.

—Why's that?

—Cos yeh can still do things with one arm. With one leg, like, yeh wouldn't be able to walk properly or anythin, but with one arm yer'd still be able to do yer normal stuff, it'd just be more awkward. Me left arm, like. Wouldn't be too bad.

—As long as I didn't have to lose me dobber I'm not bothered. Wharrabout an eye? Would yeh lose an eye? If thee gave yer a choice like, said arm or leg or eye?

Alastair closes one eye. —Yeh, that wouldn't be too bad. Still be able to see, like, wouldn't yeh? But imagine *losing* it, tho, God. Havin it gouged out. Would thee give yis an anaesthetic?

—Who?

—These people. The ones who'd be torturin yeh, like.

—Oh aye, yeh. Thee wouldn't want yeh to be in any pain while thee were rippin yer friggin eye out, like.

—In that case then yeh. It'd be me eye.

Darren looks at Alastair for a moment in what resembles disbelief then he shakes his head and looks away. —Light us up a ciggie, would yeh, Ally.

Alastair lights two, hands one to Darren who sucks hard at it and shoots smoke in a stream at the speedometer. —Ey, did I ever tell yis about me mad auntie?

—Which one?

—The one with the one eye? Me mam's sister?

—Don't think so, no.

—Aw, she was off her fuckin tree. Tellin yeh; right fuckin out of it. Born that way, but the amount a booze she put away didn't help, like. Mashed her friggin swede big time. Anyway, when I was a binlid she lost one of her beams —

—How?

—Ey?

—How'd she lose this eye?

—Dunno, can't remember. Disease or accident or somethin, I mean, she was no brawler, me auntie. But anyway thee gave her a falsie, y'know, like a glass one? Brown, cos she had brown eyes, like, but she'd always wanted blue. Really liked blue eyes, like. An it happened that another ahl girl who lived down her road had a glass eye n all but this one was blue, so me auntie used t'go round there all the time like hopin to catch this ahl queen with her eye out like so's she could skank it. Call round there of a mornin she would when this other one'd still be in bed like, her eye in a glass of water or somethin.

—That's teeth.

—What?

—Yeh put yer false *teeth* in a glass of water by the bed. Don't know what yer do with a false eye, like.

—Well, anyway, one day she did it, me auntie, managed to knock off this blue eye like, an she started wearin it instead of her proper one, but the thing was it didn't fuckin fit; it was too small. So she'd be speakin to yis, like, one brown eye workin normally an thee other one, the blue one, spinnin all over the fuckin shop in her socket. Funny as fuck, it was. When she'd get bevvied it'd roll around in her head, y'know, like a reel in a fruit machine or somethin? Fuckin boss it was. Well fuckin funny. She used to love it, tho, me auntie. Dead proud she was, to have this one blue eye whether the friggin thing fit or not. Me brother broke it tho, playin marbles, so she hadter go back to the brown one.

—Muster been off her friggin head.

—Is right.

—I had a mad auntie as well. She made me join the school footy team.

—What's so fuckin mad about that, lar?

—Nah, I mean, she didn't fuckin *make* me, I mean, she didn't tell me to or anythin, but it was cos of her that I joined.

—How?

—Well, she was dead old. A pensh. I think she was me *great*-auntie or somethin. I used to fuckin *hate* goin round there every Wednesday for tea, like, cos her insides, like, her bowels an stuff had all packed up so we'd be sittin there eatin ar scouse, like, an she'd be at thee end of the table on a friggin commode.

—Go 'way.

—Nah, it's true. Sittin there eatin yer scouse an yer scones triner ignore yer auntie shittin away as she ate her food. The noises an the smells an everythin. Used ter fuckin hate it but me mam'd make me go so I joined the school footy team cos thee used to practise on a Wednesday night on the reccy, see, so I'd have an excuse for not goin round me auntie's. Footy practice instead. So me mam just changed the visit to Thursday. Fuckin horrible. So then I had footy *and* me auntie's crappin tea. Didn't wanner join the footy team in the first friggin place, but they needed a goalie. Lost the first game eleven–nil.

Darren flicks his cigarette end out of the window.
—What the fuck's that gorrer do with bein amputated?

—What?

—That story.

—Nowt, but you were talkin about yer auntie, so . . .

—So what?

—So I talked about mine. Isn't that what we were talkin about, ar mad aunties?

—We were talkin about havin only one eye. As daft as me friggin auntie, you, Ally. No lie.

Darren shakes his head again, makes a noise somewhere between a grunt and a sigh. Mutters inaudibly and picks his nose with an index finger and rolls then flicks the bogey away, over his shoulder. Alastair's voice is low, mischievous:
—Anyway. Bet *I* know who could tell us what it's like to have only one eye.

—Oh aye? Who's that, well?

—*You* know.

—The fuck yeh talkin about, Alastair? I don't know anyone with one eye. Me auntie's dead, so what the fuck are yeh talkin about, yeh friggin divvy?

—That Blackburn supporter. The one yeh glassed in the Grapes that time.

—Aw, yer not gunner start up about that again, are yeh? Been through this a thousand fuckin times. We'd lost, cunt got gobby, I taught him a lesson. Fuckin end *of.*

—It was a bit out of order, Darren.

—Out of order? Out of fuckin order? Ey, mouth, who the fucker *you* callin out of fuckin order? Fuckin cunt mudderfucker, what gives *you* the fuckin right to call *me* out of fuckin order?

Alastair seems to shrink in his seat. Involuntary arms link across his chest some unconscious posture defensive.

—Some fuckin gob on *you*, cunt. Big as that Blackburn blert's, I mean, yeh just don't come into someone else's fuckin barrio an start shoutin the fuckin odds. *You* know that. Yeah so the cunt had his fuckin kid with him but *I* didn't know, an anyway what the fuck did he think he was doin takin his kid into an enemy alehouse? Fuckin arsehole got what he deserved. Comes into my friggin town givin it fuckin large about fuckin decline an all that shit, shadow of its former self blah blah fuckin blah, the fuck did he *think* was gunner happen? Oh yeh, mate, yer right yeh, we're all shite compared to what we used to be, fuckin fuck *that*, man. Sack that fuckin shit, lar. Not puttin up with *that* on me own fuckin turf. No one fuckin would. I mean, the fuckin money the city once had, biggest fuckin port in the world and the best fuckin team in the world bar none and then it's just skag an no jobs an every fuckin scally's gorrer piece an all the fuckin buildings fallin down an losin one—nil at home to fuckin Blackburn, I mean, shit like that fuckin *hurts*, man. An every fuckin visitor should be sensitive to that, shouldn't thee? Should have a bit of fuckin compassion, like. Cunts. Deserved everythin he fuckin well got.

The remembered red of the spurting blood and the twitching eye split like fruit and the terrified child's cries still set flame in Alastair's chest and a pounding in his skull, but nevertheless his voice is measured:

—Gettin it back now, tho, eh? People won't be able to say all that shite no more, will thee?

—Gettin *what* back?

—The, y'know, the greatness. Houllier, man. Pure fuckin genius. People'll soon start lookin at the city an thee won't see Hillsborough any more or the dockers or Jamie Bulger or the fuckin, the Spice Boys. Thee'll see victory again, won't thee? All them cups, like.

Staring ahead at the spooling road, Darren grumbles agreement.

—Is right. Pure fuckin genius the Frenchman.

—You *know* it.

Some tension eases, a tightness in the snared air slackens and a pinkness comes back to Alastair's face. As the blood slows in his body, as his pulse normalises with the adrenalin dam swinging shut. He points to a sign for Dolgellau.

—Eeyar, take the ring road, Da. Next left. Bypass that town, like.

Darren follows the instructions wordlessly and Alastair as surreptitious as he can studies Darren's face in a glance. Notes with some relief that the small stringy muscle on Darren's cheek has ceased to twitch. And that the blue ropy veins at his temple have deflated and that his knuckles on the steering wheel are now not white.

Alastair delves in the fudge box at his feet.

—Want some fudge, Da?

Headshake. Alastair eats in silence for a moment and the car swings down on to the ring road, Dolgellau grey and bunched in drizzle to the right, colossal mountain waves above holding it in permanent damp shadow, the rippled striations and torsions on those mountains like the muscling beneath pelt. Darren's voice:

—An anyway. Bastard looked like Roger Moore.

—Who did?

—That Blackburn knob'ed. Looked like Roger fuckin Moore. Same colour an everythin.

—Same colour?

—Aye, yeh. Orange-est get I've ever seen. Another reason why I lost the head.

—Ah, says Alastair, as if in some clinching realisation, some comprehension or persuasion soft and unwilled and what antidote if any to the piled burning beasts and the orders for wreckage and flesh swollen around shards? What tonic if any to the fragility of skin and the eager facility of blood to erupt and abscond? None on these steep slopes down which the sun spills shadow. None in these clouds through which the big birds soar, these winged predators eyes locked

below for any sign of life undefended, life unalert.
None in these houses, none in these busy, passing cars;
everything eats everything.

A sign:

ABERYSTWYTH

35

CITY, ABOUT TWO YEARS AGO

Some people said it came off a Colombian ship and others said a Russian and others said Chinese and still others said from Turkey, but whatever its origin in the wider world the crate of pure cocaine came up from the docks and was cut before it reached the Goree and by the time it reached Everton and Tuebrook and places it had been stepped on so many times as to render it indistinguishable from the usual poorer powders that blow perpetually around the city. Some of it, however, had found its way to Chinatown and the Dingle where in the squat flats there or the tower blocks the colour of ditchwater or in the squeezed terraces it was cooked quickly into crack and the local stores ran out of baking soda so grannies baked limp cakes and from windows on a summer evening could be heard a sound like distant small-arms fire as on numerous hobs in simmering pans the pure cocaine element was split with that distinctive cracking sound from its hydrochloric salt base and on rare occasions explosions as the volatile ether that some people used in this process ignited. Then see the reeling figures with their steaming hair and clothes. Rocked and bagged the coke from where-the-fuck found its way out into the galleries across the city, so many that if they were indicated with a red dot would give the map chickenpox, not one street gallery-free from the Dock Road to Huyton and some of these remained close to the site of landfall and so looked out on to the pagodas of Chinatown and the food smells and the music rising in through the windows continuously curtained and that's where he met Rebecca. Appearing late one night when the arguments were arriving, crisp-fried brains crunching into paranoia and despite the wrung-outness of her face, her face dark with her father's Somalian blood and the dullness of her eyes and the heavy run make-up, he looked up at that face and just thought yes. And then there was just him and her with a bag of rocks and a bottle of vodka in some high flat somewhere and they began to think of themselves in the plural and she had many clients regular and trusted and he had a kind of pure acceptance and so there was money and so there was drink and the crate of cocaine from whichever country continued to feed the city's needs and everything seemed always there so ready to hand, drugs and drink and sex and companionship it was all easy it was all sound but these were the good times and of course they couldn't last.

She returns not with crack or coke but not empty-handed; a baggie of small white pills.

—What're them?

—Temazzies. It's all I could get hold of. Make the bevvy go further, like.

—Alright.

Gulp, drink, blackout. Wake up bruised.

★ ★ ★

She returns not empty-handed.

—Did yeh gerrem? The temazzies?

—Certainly did.

—Aw, fuckin boss.

—Did yeh get the drink?

—Yep. Skanked two bottles from the Londis.

—Nice one. Great stuff.

Gulp, drink, blackout. Wake up bruised.

It can be very, very quick, sometimes. It was then.

She holds a wavering blue flame under the blackened spoon. Watching and waiting for the pills to dissolve in the bowl of the spoon and her hair hanging lankly over her face, one strand too close to the swaying flame and he lies on the bed his head pillow-propped watching through heavy-lidded eyes and waiting for that strand to catch fire. She's talking, mumbling so low that she may be addressing an imaginary figure at her shoulder or maybe even the spoon itself or the bubbling broth it contains, held so close to her drooping face.

—Five of em in care . . . five kids . . . only twenty-fucking-four I was an thee were all I had . . . if only theed've let me keep me kids . . . took five bits of *me* away thee did when thee took my children away . . .

—Rebecca.

—Somethin better than all them cunts I have to let do them things to me . . . five better things thee were . . .

—Rebecca.

—Each time takes somethin away from me . . . evry

fuckin time ... thought the last one was different like, but he was just like aller others ... when I was livin on Roscoe Street, like, an he came back with me an he liked me, he said, still fuckin gone inner mornin tho, wanny?

—Ey, Becca.

—Mean, am off the fuckin rock now ... can look after me own kids ... able to ... too right ...

She puts the spoon down on the saucer on the window sill and looks over at him. Her hair all in her face and that face beginning to tremble, shudder.

—You're different, tho, aren't yeh? Yer not like all thee others. You *like* me, don't yeh?

Slowly and in seeming pain he struggles off the bed and up into a standing position and stumbles over the floor towards her and wraps his arms, his two arms, around her skinny body and holds her there by the window high above the city, its lights aglow like fires, and he sways and they sway together as if in strong wind and his hip nudges the spoon in the saucer on the sill. Rebecca gasps and pushes him away.

—Ey! Look what yer've fuckin done! Yer spillin it, yeh soft fucking get! Fuckin leave off me!

Hottest summer for thirty years, they said. We're registering higher average temperatures than Spain or Greece, they said. Global warming, they said. Greenhouse effect. And the reaction on the soil to the reaction in the sky seemed to be among a certain social strata one strangely of hibernation, a hiding, a closing of the curtains and a pouring of drinks and a laying sweaty naked on the bed. Outside in the city car horns became more active and exhaust more choking and steel and concrete throbbed with heat and emitted parching waves, and the breeze off the Mersey when it came offered no relief bringing as it did a further wave of airless heat and the stench of rotting seaweed and bad gases popped from mud.

It was an almost unbearably hot summer, that one. Stifling days spent asleep in a dark and gasping room, temazepam-sleep, booze-sleep, two lives spent in sleep two feet apart on the bed so that slick skin did not stick to slick skin. Two deep and rhythmical breathings in a darkened choking room and only those soft sounds above the city noise beyond the ever open, always curtained window, a noise almost entirely the blare of car horns and the revving of engines. The sun sucking patience as well as strength and moisture and motivation from the sagging figures that crumpled in its heat, all that blare in the glare.

Where is he, he's in A & E. Probably the Royal Liverpool because that's the closest hospital and he's been sitting here for ages on the plastic seat, holding his left arm in his right and the hand on that left arm hangs too loose on that wrist. Terrible pain in that arm too and a lesser one in his banging head and one in his acid-burning belly also, that belly attempting to jettison bile which he chokes back down and swallows. Like a burning in his ulna and razor wire drawn tight around his skull and a clawed creature full of fighting in his stomach.

He looks around for Rebecca but among all the groaning grumbling and yelling people she isn't there.

On his left there is a man holding a blood-soaked tea towel to his eye and a big woman shrieking at him and he is threatening to punch her again and she is threatening to smack him one with another bottle again in turn and on his right a woman in a short black dress bent double clutching her belly mumbling to a nurse that she's been kicked.

—Who kicked you, love?

—*He* did . . . *im* . . .

—Who's 'he', darlin?

—*Im* . . . that *cunt* . . .

And no Rebecca. Just an image of her ducking under his flung punch all clumsy and drunk and a memory of the impact as fist hit fridge. The awful sensation of something snapping and the pain of abrupt rupture. And now the looseness of hand on wrist and the screaming and the bleeding around him in A & E it must be Friday or Saturday night he is sick in pain he needs a drink he must wait here amid this tumult until his name is called. Down here among the fuss and spillage, the threats and lungings he must wait until someone calls his name. The taste of bile and this pain, this pain.

Back to Rebecca's through the park. Early morning so not too hot yet and traffic only a trickle and birds singing, small brown birds in the trees he knows not their names only that their songs have been scraped from his veins. The plaster on his arm still moist and so white, bone white as if his left forearm is made entirely of bone, denuded of all flesh or as if the muscle itself has ossified. Or swollen like Popeye's, twice the size of his bicep.

The light of the day is heavy, oppressive. Such a weight of light, hot and leaden on his soggy head. And a honed quality to it too, against which he must squint, narrow his eyes, seek only to shut it out.

And all he wants to do is drink and sleep, in that order. Have a drink then fall asleep with Rebecca close by him but he vaguely recalls trying to hit her so he picks a bunch of yellow flowers at the edge of the pond, the scummed surface dotted with cans and bags sun-bleached and when he has reached Rebecca's flat the flowers have drooped and wilted but he still presents them to her when she opens the door to his meek knock. And she even smiles, her face swollen with sleep and hangover, her lips cracked and claggy with thick white paste and her eyes in puffed slits, this face even smiles as she takes the flowers.

—Can I come in?

—Yer arm broke, is it?

—Aye.

—Serves yeh right, well.

—Can I come in?

She waves him in with the flopping flowers and he enters and collapses exhausted into a chair. The flat is just as he left it; sweet smell of stale cheap Scotch and stale fag smoke and something meaty as if sausages have been recently fried. Every curtain closed still and he can barely see Rebecca, only the drifting pale blue of her stained, frayed dressing gown as she puts the flowers in a beaker of water and puts that on top of the television.

—Djer like em? The flowers, like?

—Yeh, ther lovely. But ther weeds, y'know.

Dandelions. Yer've brought me wee-the-beds. Useter say as a kid that if yeh picked one yer'd piss the bed.

She turns to him and touches his face and he must look sad to her because she tells him not to look that way and sits by him and lights a cigarette.

—It's alright, don't worry. Ther lovely, honest. I've always liked dandelions an it's me fave colour, yellow is. An anyway, who decides what's a weed an what isn't? All's it is is somethin out of place. I mean, say yer had a field of nettles, right, an a rose started to grow there, then *that* would be the weed. The rose. Knowmean? A weed is just a plant growin where yeh don't want it to grow. That's all it is.

She kisses him on the cheek.

—So ta very much. Ther dead nice. An ther not weeds in here, are thee? In here ther flowers. How's thee arm?

He rubs the place where her lips touched his skin.

—Not bad. Thee gave me some boss painkillers. An why yeh in such a good mood? I thought yer'd still have a massive cob on.

—Me? Nah. Always happy, me. Cheery soul. Wait there.

She goes into the bedroom and returns with a small brown bottle. Shows him the label: methadone in a liquid suspension.

—Where djer get that?

—Mally. Malachi.

—Oh, *him*. That sleazy bastard. Whatjer have to let im do to yeh for him to give yeh that?

—Yeh don't wanner know. An I don't wanner remember. An anyway djer wanner get wrecked or not? Fuckin face on yeh, Jesus. Got us some friggin gear, didn't I? Least yeh could do is fuckin smile abahr it, Jesus. Did it for *you*, y'know, for us, like, so we could get wrecked together. Djer want to or not? Do it on me own like, if you're not up for it. Makes no odds.

—Still got that whisky?

—Some of it, yeh. Most of it.

He nods and lights up a cigarette. Rebecca unscrews bottles. Scrape of tin against grooved glass.

He awakes in wet. Rebecca is snoring beside him and the room is tar dark and he is wet from the waist down, wet and cold. The plaster on his arm glows almost luminous in the blackness and with his good arm he reaches down under the covers and dabbles his fingers in the moisture and raises them to his nose and sniffs: piss. His or Rebecca's he doesn't know, maybe both of theirs mingled on and in the mattress but it doesn't matter, he doesn't care, wrecked and weary enough to sleep in piss he is and he does.

The dandelions soon begin to decay. Droop in defeat in the heat in the room, the dark and choking hot room, scorched traffic noise outside in the blinding day eye-searing and the flowers' green turns pale and their yellow turns black and left like that in the stagnant tap water they soon enough start to stink. On top of the TV always on, on top of Kilroy Trisha and Ricki their heads hang over the photographs of children, five framed photographs arranged in a row and the curls of petals desiccated and browning detach and drift down across those framed faces, see-saw across those frozen faces flat under glass and come to rest around them as if shed by those images themselves, as if elemental of the falling of family, not flower. About nine, the oldest child would be; he is seven in the photograph.

And these hot days spent blurred and wasted yet not wasted since waste was the aim. The heat's clamp on the face, that grip relaxed with the hiss of each opened can of beer, with each sizzle of bubbles in a glass as stolen gin or vodka or whisky was mixed and with the potential that each embarkation on a booze cruise proclaimed, the small sticky room widening, expanding, the recession of oppression spatial and climatic and historical and social and other, so much other. Those ostensive and demonstrable and those poorly paraphrased only in the notion that within the battering of cells continuous resides some secret. A gift, even. Some sort of affliction so that the sufferer wanders holy through the heated hectic world alone among the fever in conversing with ghosts and Christ and the Reaper himself and still further, each drink an address to the blank and averted visage of God. Soaked days and drenched nights when slurring and stumbling masked the true meaning of the quest which was some connection close and clean to the universe's inaccessible truths and that the drinking was something somehow divine, some wild spinning around a centre still and sparkling which was the condition of being chosen, just chosen. And the secret knowing that to move like this amid spew and bruising was to be truly and only in this way awfully alive.

The glow of the plastered arm in the crackling

blackness as glass was raised to lip. A woman's abandoned laughter, in the direction of the kitchen, and the ripe reek of the flowers in rot.

There's an old pisshead on the steps of the RC cathedral, opposite Mountford Hall. An old pisshead, a screamer, eyes yellow and skin scratched raw because of the bad salts in his blood and his face turned by years of alcohol and exposure into a road map. He's sucking on a half-bottle of Buckfast and bellowing at a group of Chinese students who ignore him and he bellows abuse at their backs then turns to the lone figure approaching him.

—Hi, you! Broken-arm! C'mer!

The figure, one arm in plaster, does.

—Brek yer fuckin arm, av yeh, al brek yer fuckin neck! Fuckin neck, cunt!

—Hiya, Dad.

—Brek yer fuckin neck, lad! Scared no fucker me!

—What yis after, Dad? Yeh want some money?

The old pisshead takes the offered coins and puts them in his pocket.

—Fuck off with yer fuckin money! Doan need yer fuckin charity, brek yer fuckin neck, cunt!

—Alright. See yis later, well.

—Gwahn, fuck off!

He does.

—Ey, c'mer! C'mer, you! You with the fuckin broken arm, fuckin c'mer, will yeh!

He ignores the shouting and only once turns back at the corner of Oxford Street to see the old wetbrain tiny beneath the vast cathedral, a small shouting shape in the sunlight as if dragged into madness by the spiked and glittering enormity at his back, then he turns down Oxford Street into Mulberry Street sweat seeping into his unwashed clothes and enters the cool welcome gloom of the pub there. Straight up to the bar at which Rebecca sways.

—How long yeh been here?

She holds up her glass, half empty. —*That* long.

—But yer fuckin out of it. Holdin out on me, are yeh?

—No, fuck off. Saved yeh some. Mazzies.

He attempts to order a drink but Rebecca slides off her stool and the barman ejects them so they walk home, he holding Rebecca up the long way down Crown Street so as to avoid the RC cathedral and the old screamer who may still be there and also to pay a visit to one of the shops by the university, free of perspex barriers with it being a student area and thus easy to steal from. He buys four cans of lager and robs a bottle of MD2020, strawberry-flavoured bright red syrup like some sort of chemical waste, by-product, run-off. The stronger stuff's behind the counter.

Out of the heat back at home Rebecca attempts to cook the temazepam into injectable form but she cannot even hold the spoon steady so he does it for her while she curls into a ball on the couch and tells him about a dream she had last night in which Stuart the father of her first child appeared to her out of a swirling silver mist and told her in a tone of immeasurable gentleness to drop everything and leave it all and simply run away.

★　★　★

—Becca. You've gorrer do it for me. You've gorrer jag it.

—Fuck off.

—Becca, yer've *got* to. The plaster, like: Can't stick it in me left arm an can't use that hand either. Just can't do it. You've gorrer do it for me.

—Alright, well. C'mer. Pain inner fuckin arse, you.

He wakes suddenly in the middle of the night or perhaps at noon only the sun has imploded and the blackness is almost total. Sitting upright extremities a-tremble sweat running down into his panting mouth black and hot and a terror on him hammering his heart a shape of pure evil at the foot of the bed this heat this darkness this isolation he knows awaits him for ever and ever and ever. He is whining he is keening he is mewling his hair on end his skin crawling never a terror as total as this, dangled over vast abyss pure nothingness negation never-ending scum, lowest wretch on the earth.

The evil shape hisses and darts at his face and he screams.

—Sa marrer? S fuckin shoutin?

—Aw, Becca . . . you've gorrer fuckin help me here, Becca . . .

He launches himself sideways and thuds on to the floor and crawls on all fours naked across that floor plugging each empty can and bottle he finds to his lips. Noise like a rusty hinge creaking in his seared and leaping throat and his arse like his plastered arm, glow-stick white in the darkness.

A light snaps on but the evil does not leave. It just scurries up to the dirty ceiling to dangle there by its feet.

—Sa fuckin marrer? Sall a fuckin . . .

He crawls back up on to the bed gabbling pleading nonsense words his face all red at Rebecca's. I've got the fear, he seems to gibber, take this fear away from me. She pushes him and his voice away and sits up slow, unsteady, scans the room with swollen eyes and squints at the syringe on the floor. Recognition eventually arrives and she picks it up, shakes it; liquid in the barrel although she knows not how or why, does not recall passing out before she or he could take this hit, she only knows that this will stop the noise. She reaches for the flailing arm at her side, the thrashing plastered arm, holds it still and jabs the needle into the skin above the top edge of the plaster in a vague vein area and pushes the plunger and takes the needle out and down with her into some form of sleep and he instantly does the same, all panic dispelled, all gone horror, both of them back down into their own peculiar blacknesses before either one can realise that the spike has snapped and left its tiny tip in a vein. Instant stillness there is, two wax mannequins supine and snoring on the bed just a settling spring in the mattress sounding strangely like a snigger.

Something crunches beneath his feet.

—The fuck's that?

He steps off, sees the plastic syringe cracked.

—Aw shit.

Checks the sole of his foot for wounds and there is none. Gathers the bits of broken barrel and chucks them out the window into the back alley.

★　★　★

—When's that plaster comin off?

—Coupla weeks, I think. Maybe three.

—Yer sure?

—Yeh. Why?

—Cos it looks like it's been rubbin against yer arm. Look, there, on thee inside of yer elbow. See where it's all gone red? Must be rubbin against it, irritatin it like. Berrer gerrit seen to.

—Nah, it's fine. Bit itchy, like, that's all.

—Beginnin to niff a bit as well, to be honest with yis. That can't be right.

—Nah, it's fine. Gets a bit sweaty under there, like, that's all it is.

—Does it hurt?

—Wee bit, I suppose. Like a sting or a bite or somethin.

—See? Get to the fuckin doc's, well, will yeh.

—Nah, it's fine. Stop yer worryin.

—Well, it's *your* fuckin arm.

—Is right. So shurrup an stop worryin.

Like an inverted boil, a carbuncle in reverse, small hollow red depression on the inside of the elbow occasionally hidden beneath the plaster-of-Paris edge depending on what position the arm is in. Crimson discoloration on the lip of this crater beginning to blacken inside at the pit where the tiny spike digs out decay, steel seed sprouting sepsis. Necrosis of the living tissue starting at cellular level this blueprint in miniature for war or indeed even life itself all curdling to carrion. Small suppurant rupturing beginning to boil around the foreign body and whatever invaders infinitesimal it infects the flesh with pre-fevered with things other yet still augmented by this spore of putrefaction, this plague grain, this ulcer oat splitting into blackly blooming shoots.

—Gerroff me. I mean it; fuckin gerraway from me. Don't come anywhere near me, will yeh.

—Why? What's wrong? Wharrav I fuckin done now?

—Yer've started to fuckin stink is what yer've done.

—I've just gorrout the friggin shower!

—Don't care. Yer pure rank. I'm tellin yeh, it's that fuckin arm; it honks. I've been tellin yeh for weeks, it's goin friggin rotten. Doesn't it fuckin hurt? It *must* fuckin hurt to smell that bad.

—A bit, yeh. Kinda burns.

—Well, there y'are then. That's not good. Get to the fuckin doc's.

—I've gorrer go there in about a week anyway to av the plaster off. Might as well ask im about it then, mightn't I?

—Up to you. But yeh not comin anywhere near me with that bad fuckin stink hangin round yis. I'm serious. Smell like a fuckin farmyard yeh do.

—It's them dead flowers. Why don't yeh chuck em away?

—It's not them flowers it's *that* fuckin arm. Yeh makin me sick.

—Ah fuck off, well.

—Where yeh goin?

—Pub.

—Good. Al be able to fuckin breathe again for a change.

★   ★   ★

Like an active volcano, seen from above. Black slopes rising to a jelly-textured lip of leprous white encircling a depth of seething scarlet. Black tentacles like veins in negative wrapped around the wasting muscle in the tight and humid darkness beneath the plaster spreading outwards from the putrid pit and the bubbling pus popping vaporous release, reek of rot and sea-dredged slime from silt and mud age-old. Stink and taint of not simply expiration but mortification, a festering strafing the blood and not only that but a creeping carbuncle too aimed at the labouring heart. Crawling corrosion and stink of shit from the still-living limb, gangrene canker flesh-churning. This raging wound a spyhole to the soul and its diseased heat, the red rank wretchedness present in every cell and the moribund promise in all mere movement. The tiny tip of metal a claw in the marrow, underscoring claw of the debased state that such smallness can create such rampant blight. The arm was lost from the moment it flailed in a loud and bloodied room and curled to cover the blue and bawling face.

—Wharrer yeh doin on the floor?

   —I'm in agony. I'm in fuckin agony.

—Aw fuck off.

—Me arm . . . me fuckin arm . . . I'm in fuckin agony, Rebecca . . .

   —What did I friggin tell yeh? I *told* yeh. Should a gone the doc's when I told yeh to, shouldn't yeh?

   —An ambulance . . . call me a fuckin ambulance . . .

—Alright, but I don't see what good that will do: you're an ambulance.

—Call me a fucking ambulance, Rebecca!

—Call it yeh fuckin self. I'm not yer fuckin slave. Should a listened to me, shouldn't yeh, but no, you knew best. There's a phone box outside an while yer there skank us a bottle from thee offy like yeh said yis were goin to cos I've just necked the last. Go ed. An stop yer fuckin screamin, will yeh? Neighbours'll hear. Move yer fuckin arse, go on. Tampin for a fuckin drink here I am.

—Me arm . . . I'm dyin . . . it's fuckin agony . . .

—Gerroff yer fuckin arse!

And once we learned how to hew from the soil that element which will return us to that mulch. Coaxed steel shaped to render flesh and bone-break, what we are parting before what we do. As if in a hatred self-centred and vast we tease and tinker that under which we buckle, bend and come apart as if the execration is too big to bear as if there is a need to prove this frailty. The rumour of simple disintegration requiring rude proof, the metal in the muscle, the rot in the bone, the stench and suppuration in the still-living skin, the seeable and smellable image in the world of the black putrefaction in the beating heart and so this welcome for metal. The cold cone nosing through the blood hungry to puncture those shadowy chambers and them just yearning to yield.

There is a bright white light too bright to bear and a man in a white coat not quite as bright.

—Can you see me?

Nod.

—Can you hear me?

Nod.

Then there is pain and in this pain this bright man explaining the necessity of arresting the necrosis and talk of luck and cell death and irreparable damage and trauma and luck again and advances in prostheses and some darkness close to reaching the heart and great improvements in artificial-limb technology and really no reason why an amputee cannot live a normal life like everyone else full and content. Then this bright figure bends over him and places a hand gently on his rising chest.

—I'll leave you now. Get some sleep. When you wake up there'll be, erm, other people to see you.

Sleep.

Then two tall men in black flanking the bed.

—Can you hear me?

Nod.

—Can you see me?

Nod.

Then there is pain and in that pain these two dark men talking of a collapse in an off-licence while in the process of stealing a bottle of whisky for which an arrest is to be made along with twenty-eight other similar offences each of these supported by CCTV evidence and also the theft of three prescription pads from three different surgeries these too supported by CCTV evidence. Specific places, specific dates. No need to say anything but case could be harmed if you fail to say anything now which you later rely on in a court of law do you understand these rights do you wish to say anything?

Nod.

—What?

Nod.

—What is it you wish to say?

Nod.

—Still out of it by the looks. Leave him. He's not goin anywhere.

—Yeh. We will be back for you. Understand?

Nod.

—Won't need the handcuffs for this one, will we?

—Nah. Just a cuff.

—Yeh.

Nod nod nod nod nod nod nod nod nod nod.

Sleep.

She was never to be seen again, Rebecca. Terrible days alone and unwhole except for an accidental visit by an acquaintance called Quockie who had come to the hospital to see someone else and had recognised the pale face on the pillow above the unbalanced mismatched body shape beneath the starchy bedclothes. But just that one brief visitation from the outside, no other, until the two dark men return with a tale of untraceable family and next-of-kinlessness and then they are each side of him as he moves, his whole arm being gripped tight guiding him through long white corridors and out into an interval of sunlight and then into a car and then he is in that car as it moves and then he is in a police station and then he is in a cell. Never to be seen again, Rebecca.

Three people, two men and a woman, elevated behind a long wooden bench. Three faces frowning, six arms folded and a man addressing these figures and gesturing towards but not looking at the bandaged shape to his right and VICTIM is the word he likes to use. VICTIM of addiction he says VICTIM of gangrene VICTIM of a traumatic operation VICTIM of a cruel and self-serving partner VICTIM of a broken family and abusive father VICTIM. Then talk of a discharge, more talk of discharge this one this time an abstraction conditional on the accused seeking help for his addictions already suffered enough a clinic for this purpose free to go lessons learned hope you can rebuild your life custodial sentence suspended contingent on successful completion of rehabilitation course.

Free to go where?

To a big building in a big garden. Then a room in that big building. Then lots of people their faces ideograms of sadness and rue and lots of talk and tears and tantrums and a stern and scowling man called Peter Salt. Then long thin dry longing days as the summer died and rain fell and then eventual release. An empty head and an empty breast and an empty sleeve flapping release.

There's a peephole in the door. That's a new addition. Probably a new lock as well but he puts his old key in and it fits and turns and the door swings open and he steps inside and it is just as he left it; the gloom and the smells and the scatter. He closes the door behind him.

—Rebecca? It's me. Are yis in?

No response.

—Rebecca?

Unoccupied the flat, no telly blaring, that still sensation of emptiness. He enters the front room, sees some burst and battered trainers big enough to belong to a male propped up against the blank telly screen and on top of that telly a glass containing some thin grey mush green-furred with mould and under that glass and held down by it a stack of paper money finger-thick. He lifts the glass up off the notes and places it on the floor then takes the money and spreads it in a loose fan on the floor and sees fives and tens and twenties and even a couple of fifties like a foreign currency to him, he looks around over each shoulder as if in search of some standing silent watcher then bundles the money up into a roll and stands and stuffs it in his pocket and quickly leaves, all these actions carried out mono-limbed with the half-arm mirroring each movement of the whole one in deficient imitation or as if that truncated limb is actually growing and sentient and learning from its more developed neighbour. Outside he scurries down the side street towards the main road and drops his keys down a drain and stiffens instantly as he hears someone call his name and turns to face the caller or callers. Quockie and that twat Malachi. Approaching him fast. Standing in front of him so close he can smell beer on their breaths.

—This you just out of thee ozzy then?

—Yeh. Yesterday.

Malachi is gawping at the loose and empty sleeve.

—Fuck me, lar, what happened to thee arm?

Quockie turns to him. —I told yeh, he lost it. Didn't
I tell yeh he'd had it taken off?

—Fuckin hell, man. Bad news. What's it like?

Quockie shakes his head and turns away from
Malachi. —Listen. You lookin for Rebecca?

—Yeh.

—Well, yer not gunner find her. She's done one.

—Where to?

—Fuck knows, but she's in big fuckin trouble. She'll
be lucky to get herself out of *this* one, tellin yeh.

Malachi nods. —Oh aye. Double fucked she is, lar,
no lie. Wanner know what she did?

Some grin on Malachi's face. —Only gone an
screwed Tommy fuckin Maguire, hasn't she? Jacked a
twelve-year-old kid in Stanley Park. Saw the soft get
countin his swag on the fuckin swings like, an wellied
him one an skanked the dough.

Quockie nods. —Is right. An guess wha? This kid
was only one of Tommy's friggin couriers, wanny?

—Oh aye. Only one of Tommy's fuckin little mules,
like, that's all.

—Oh fuck. Jesus Christ.

—Is right. Malachi leans in, voice dropped, grinning.
—An that's not all. She fuckin well went n called
Tommy an blamed the whole bleedin thing on *you*.

—Yeh. Quockie drops his voice too. —Listen, yer've
gorrer do one. Fuckin leg it, man. Leave. Get as far
away from town as possible.

—Where to? Where the fuck should I go?

—Christ, *I* don't fuckin know, do I? Just fuckin anywhere, man.

Malachi laughs. —New fuckin Zealand won't be far enough, lar.

—Put a pin in a fuckin map an go there. Soon as yeh can, just fuck off. Tommy knows yer've just ad yer arm off an he's lookin to take thee other one, honest, just get yerself down Lime Street and gerron the next train out. Bunk it if yer have to, but just fuckin disappear.

He is running already.

A memory:

One among many as a boy being taken away with his brothers and sisters by his mother to various unknown towns to escape the booted roar that was his dad. Towns on the Wirral at first then North Wales then deeper into that land and all of them huddled in B & Bs and the smell of chips and hands sticky with lemonade or juice and fighting each other on the bed and the mother at the window looking out at these strange towns and chain-smoking. And then standing outside a phone box and the tearful conversation going on inside the glass box and then the train journey back northwards but this abiding memory of one of those places hills and sea and promenade he searched for crabs beneath the pier and found four and also fifty pence he fed chips to seagulls and ate candyfloss and swam out of his depth in the sea and the people around him spoke a different language but one he'd heard a few times in shops and streets in his home city. The only place he tantrummed against leaving there were mountains around it like a vast security fence and what was that place what was its name?

—Mum, why's that man only got one arm?
—What man, love?
—That man over there, lookin at the map. See him?
—Maybe he had an accident.
—But why hasn't he got two arms tho?
—I don't know. Now stop staring, it's rude.

Pigeons squabbling over a dropped sarnie on the station platform. One flaps away with a large chunk of cheese on to the top of the train and two more follow it and continue to fight, dirty wings thrashing, screeching, stabbing. This violent competition always, always. Perpetual attempts to sap strength and steal light and rip roots and choke and strangle and smother, some war always inescapable this smug and squalid subjugation. Thin ice beneath and an eggshell veneer above, such frail fortresses against the attendant distemper.

The pigeon drops the cheese and flaps away and as the others fight over the food a little bird darts in and scoops it up and takes it up into the high rafters of the distant station roof. Little bird, fist-sized, substantial splash of red. He thinks it may be a robin.

There is mist outside the windows, the train is moving through mist and in that mist there is a marsh and beyond that an estuary and beyond that mountains, the tops of which appear out of this sinking mist as if revealing themselves consciously. As if in the very act of being created they appear in the distance out of this thin fog. Out of his recall too they soar unchanged, unaltered from his memory, massive presence always there, of that he is now aware.

Directly opposite the station is a cheap hotel. Soon he is on a bed in a sparse room with a local directory on his knees because the bar beneath his room is sending up a dangerous stink and a dangerous noise and the very first entry in the book is his — the double A.

And then a great elapsing. Then a tremendous surrender in which the sounds of the sea become like food and he dreams of Tommy coming out of the waves, a fat Neptune in a perm and a shellsuit with the eyes of a squid. Tommy in the streets, Tommy in the shops, Tommy at AA, Tommy in the dole office. A time in which he lived in dread of a knock at his door and a time which he will one day come to wish he could remember more of, a wide settling, a diffuse calm, and too the time before that of a lost frenzy, an intensity flashes past only when the sun is hot or the smell of rotting vegetation or meat is around or when somewhere outside the window in the narrow streets of this small seaside town a siren erupts into sudden and desolate pain. Or the ghost of the limb still working beyond his stump and the pain in there the pitch of which sometimes exceeds the stimulus and brews up a nerve storm characterised by spontaneous movement and jactitation and cold surface temperature to the skin and sweating and a reduction in blood flow and in the space beneath this hurricane of sensation resides a permanent reminder of that gone fever, those over-heated days, he wishes the arm was still there and nothing reminds him of nothing, what's gone recalls what's gone and he becomes capable of living with that and it suits him now just fucking fine. But the night sweats are bad when it seems like he's still exuding alcohol and the sizzle of the sea is a low-hiss accompaniment to his lost life and the gone carnage but he's generally glad he ended up here, he knows this as he tugs the food from his garden soil or watches the fox nose through the hedge or sniffs its lingering musk or feeds celery to his rabbit or watches the wild birds eat the seeds he's left out for them in the morning sun and the unworried disconnection he held so dear echoes within the language around him:

Aberystwyth: mouth of the river

Eryri: place of eagles

Pontrhydfendigaid: bridge near the ford of the Blessed Virgin.

And Rebecca? What of her? Never that agog for life, he only hopes she's still spending most of her days in sleep. Awake, she was open to torment and sometimes it's like he hears her voice drifting from some other shore and calling and calling and trying to teach him the skills to listen because he simply can't hear her but without her in that past, and with two entire arms, he knows he'd be working in some shitty factory some-where or stacking shelves in a supermarket in days of hate and deafness all dull and without story, all that, her, it made him what he is, the uniqueness of a woman and an addiction and a snapped and dirty needle and catastrophic cell death, all of this his ink.

Almost every morning, the one-eyed fox comes down off the mountain. The old one-eyed fox, down off the hill and into his garden, there to sniff and spray. And the birds come down from the trees and the sky to eat his seeds; sent down on scythes of sunlight they too appear and eat his seeds.

SUPERMARKET 2

I did it all, I did. Everythin yeh care to name. Don't remember where or how it began, it just seems to have always been there; I mean, I don't recall the first spliff or the first bevvy or whatever, it was just always there. Part of me, like. An I did fuckin everythin, the whole spectrum, the gamut; spliff then speed then acid then mushies then E then charlie then crack then skag then temazzies an diazzies an methadone an Mogadon an Demerol an pethidine an ephedrine an Dexedrine an Benzedrine, all different kinds of opiates, everything designed to annul all pain. I blacked out in poky, smoky rooms, the walls lined with other blacked-out people. And booze; God how I attacked the booze, beers an Concorde wine an Thunderbird an Merrydown cider an Spesh an brandy an vodka an whisky an rum an gin an Martini an cooking sherry an everythin, everything. One time even meths, a handkerchief wrapped over the end of the bottle to filter out thee emetic, the mild poison that makes yeh vom. And so many combinations of all these things, so many variations to try; the nuances of each hit didn't matter really, thee never do, just as long as thee spin yer brain sideways. That's all that counts.

An here it all is, here in thee alcohol aisle. Rows, racks of it, higher than my head. No spirits here; they're kept behind the counter at the ciggie booth, to deter thieves like, but here all spread out before me is the beer an the wine, so much fuckin wine, an the sherry an the more exotic stuff like Kahlua an cream liqueur an stuff like that. I carry me basket between these rows, wine on me right an beer to me left, this drink seeming to emit a heavy hum, not unpleasant like, more enticing, beguiling. So fuckin easy it would be to buckle in thraldom here, let that hum buzz in me skull. So easy. So lovely. Just fall an give in to what these stacked racks offer an promise, the mad excitement in them, their taste secondary really to the questions that that first sip would demand, questions intense enough to hammer yer heart an flail yer brain an make yer balls retreat back up into yer thorax. What's gunner happen to me? Where will I be tomorrow? Who will I be with? Out of the million possibilities in the night ahead which ones will befall me?

Which is why I always preferred the booze. Mixed with uppers, yeh, sound, superb, but thee opiates: nah. Not for me. Temazepam worked for me, Christ yeh, the madness in it when mixed with the bevvy, but skag an methadone n stuff, there's nowt of life in those drugs, no enhancement, just a steady sleep, a surrendering, a giving-in. Lust for life? Fuck off; it's a lust for death. But the bevvy, tho, the drink; drink steadily for days, weeks, eat an sleep little an yeh eventually reach this wide an shining place, yeh stride through an that place is outside but also in yer head and yer heart an in that place you can be a god. You soar. You commit atrocities with impunity and yer mind frisks an leaps around the guilt you easily drown an there is a tremendous strength inside yeh cos yeh know, fuck yes yeh *know*, that this is not for the weak, no way, to be a drunk takes not just desperation but a kind of bright an gleaming courage. And a strength and a commitment incomprehensible to non-drunks, those strange straight figures vaguely drifting through yer spotlit world, those brittle upright shapes at thee edge of your conscious-ness reduced into uselessness by their acceptance, their lack of adventure, their neglect and fear of thee endless quest for joy. They know fuckin *nothing* of that. They sleep an rise and eat an shit an mumble an *work*, that's their main fuckin thing, thee *work*, slave at some spirit-sapping soul-sucking obligation until thee start dying in increments an while they're checkin their watches for their precious fuckin dinner hour I'm walkin into the just-opened pub, the smell of polish an the wood an brass an glass all gleaming an the sun slantin in through the windows, swirling motes in the beams. How do thee live without it, those people? What do thee fill the gaping socket with? Me an Rebecca walkin into that pub an the money in ar pockets an the poor fuckin fools outside an the head on the first beer an the whisky chaser an the taste of that the pure fuckin

come back

return

okay

to this fuckin wasteland of sobriety post-booze. Court-coerced drunk in the clinic an what do yeh do once yer released, sober amputee in this wasteland? You plant seeds in the soil, that's what yeh do. You dig potato drills in the desert an leave nuts out for the birds who from now on will do your flying for yeh.

And you read. You open negotiations with words.

But that's booze, that's what it is. That. Is. Alcohol. Alcohol is all the magic drawn from yer days, yer drudgery, it is every last one of yer wishes distilled. Yer desires aged in oak, like. It is yer cells swimming in tingling soup it is the true essence of everyday objects revealing itself to only you it is all you've ever longed for it is transport it is ecstasy it is

SO ALIVE

alcohol it is shitting yer kex in shops it is spewing blood in people's faces it is loosened teeth blacked eyes broken noses it is yer arm stinking as it rots on yer body it is agony it is filled with shit and pus it is

shame/blame/disgust

it is to be fucked and forgotten just gerrout of this fuckin place.

I take me basket to one of the tills an wait in line. My pretty Onion Girl is the second person before me an I watch as she places her shoppin on the conveyor belt; the usual staples – bread, milk, cheese, pasta, rice – and fruit an vegetables an that ham-an-pineapple pizza an a packet of fish fingers. A healthy selection, an just look at me now, this is what I worry about now, these are thee immediate concerns of me days, about the mucoid-provoking properties of full-fat milk, about trapped wind, about why there is sensation where there is no limb. About fertilisers. About the health of a rabbit. About soil pH an whether there'll be enough rain. About slug an snail repellents; to kill or not to kill? Pellets an salt, or eggshells an beer traps? About what to leave out for my one-eyed fox. About

149

an unexpected knock on me door. About which foods or vitamins will best assist the healing process which goes on an on an will remain ongoing until the day I die an begin to rot, a state I know something about already. The living being decaying away.

I put me shoppin on the belt an the lady on the till notices me empty sleeve an rings for a bagger an he comes an bags me stuff up into one bag as I pay. Take me shoppin an leave, the wind a bit stronger, rain still holdin off but the sky gettin darker n darker. A huge black-bellied cloud. Sky-whale. Leviathan above. Bit of a thirst on me now; could do with some coffee. Down to the caff on the prom, I reckon, before headin home. Yep, that's me plan.

Step 7: We humbly asked Him to remove our shortcomings. And then laughed at the impossibility of the task and also in embarrassment, the submissive nature and posture of this request so at odds with the swaggering invincibility we were trying to painfully relinquish and the laughter grew an grew an became uncontrollable, hysterical and ar eyes bulged in horror and ar skins paled and ar pulses raced yet still we laughed, we hid arselves an held ar heads an put ropes around ar necks or razors to ar wrists an ar faces dripped with tears an still we laughed, laughed so hard that ar larynxes ruptured an what came out was screams an blood. But still we were laughing; we may have looked an sounded like we were in tremendous anguish, indescribable pain but no, this was laughter. Honest; we were amused.

CAR

—I spy with my little eye, somethin beginnin with . . . M.

—M, is it? Oo now let me guess. It wouldn't be fuckin *mountain*, now, would it?

Alastair shakes his head. —No.

—No? Not mountain? Yer sure?

—Yep.

—Oh, I know wharrit is; it's 'meff', innit? Yer've just caught sight of yerself in the wing mirror so the word is 'meff'.

—Not that either.

—What then? Just friggin tell us, will yeh, cos I'm gettin bored now.

—Mynydd.

—Eh? What the fuck's that?

Alastair grins. —It's 'mountain' in Welsh.

—Aw, fuck off, that doesn't count. Gorrer be a language both of us can speak or there's no fuckin point. An anyway I *said* 'mountain' first time so fuck right off.

—A draw, then, that one. My turn again. I spy –

—Nah, fuck that, lad. Yer disqualified.

—What for?

—Unfair an Inappropriate Language Useage. It's a proper rule, like.

—Who says?

—No one, it just is. Gorrer use a language both players can understand or it defeats the whole fuckin purpose. So yeh lost that one an now it's my turn: S.

—S?

—Yeh. I spy with my little eye somethin beginnin with S.

—Stream.

—No.

—Sky.

—No.

—Signpost.

—No. An am bored of it now so al tell yeh: soft-shite-on-me-left-who-won't-stop-playin-this-stupid-fuckin-game-an-borin-me-fuckin-shitless. Which is *you*, by the way, in case yeh can't work it out. Game over, I won.

—Sound. Stupid friggin game anyway.

—*You* started it.

—Didn't.

—Yeh, yer did, back by that fuckin farm. Somethin beginnin with P, you said, an it was 'poo' on the road. That was thee answer, like. So it was your fuckin idea to play the fuckin game. You started it, Alastair.

—Didn't.

—Yeh fuckin well *did*, lad.

—Didn't.

—Did.

—A million more 'didn't's than you say 'did's.

—A million an *one*.

—Infinity.

—Fuck off. How far now?

—Dunno. Not far. Nuther half-hour or so.

—Jesus. Been drivin for fuckin hours. Gunner have to make a bog stop soon, I'm burstin.

They enter a valley, a thin strip of road less than halfway up its southern slope. To the right this slope rises sheer up to huge knives and chisels of rain-carved wind-whittled rock that slash and score the grey and sullen sky and occasionally slice boulders off and on to the road below, car-sized rock barrels which elephant down the valley wall and across the road and come to desolate rest in the thalweg which presently along with scores of these huge rocks bears testament to a recent flash flood, the warty writhing branches of the naked trees snagged with empty and torn fertiliser bags and fence posts trailing tentacles of wire and other smaller trees uprooted and the carcass of what was probably once a sheep, what flesh remains just sludge on the bones bough-caught and dangling, clanking in the wind, this loose and lolling skeleton some hideous mobile, wind-chime plaything of a demon or a god displeased and demented.

Alastair sniffs up. —Ew. What's that niff? Have yeh farted?

—Yeh. Darren nods. —Can't help it. I'm burstin. Must be that friggin battered sausage.

—*What* fuckin battered sausage? You had a battered sausage in Bala?

Darren nods.

—Snidey get, why didn't *I* gerrer fuckin battered sausage? Kept *that* one friggin quiet, didn't yeh?

—Aye, cos I know thee effect it would've had. Every time you have a battered sausage, lar, yeh can fart for fuckin Liverpool. An I'm stuck in this friggin car with yeh.

—Says *you*! Fuckin Stinkarse here! Christ, that fuckin *mings*. Alastair pulls the neck of his trackie up over his nose. —It smells like fresh shit.

—Well, that's exactly wharrit is, innit? It's gas, like. Poo gas. Little particles of shite floatin around in thee air an you've just breathed some in. Surprised yeh can't taste it, lar. Yeh dirty fuckin get.

—I didn't fuckin well *want* to, did I? Had no friggin choice in the matter, yeh smelly bastard.

—Can't hear yeh, lad, yer voice's all muffled. Pull yeh top down below yer chin.

—Fuck off.

Alastair winds his window down and Darren laughs and turns up a side road little wider than the Morris itself, hedges on each side clawing at the wings. He pulls up next to a gate and turns the engine off.

—Wharrer yeh doin?

—Pull that fuckin trackie down, will yeh? Can't hear a word yer sayin.

Alastair does. —Wharrer yeh doin?

—I'm gunner have a shite in that field there. I'll do it in me kex if I don't.

—Wharrabout bog roll?

—Oh aye, yeh. Fuck. Eeyar, pass that road atlas, will yeh?

Alastair does and Darren flicks through the pages to the map of Manchester and its environs and winks at Alastair as he rips those two pages out and crumples them up, smooths them out again, recrumples them.

—What yeh doin that for?

—It makes the paper softer, like, more comfy on yer arse. Have a fuckin ringpiece like a blood orange if I don't. See yis in a minute.

He leaves the car and slams the door and Alastair watches him vault the gate and disappear behind a hedge. Sheep bleating and the whine of wind up the valley and off the toothed tops of its walls and around the ticking car. Alastair winds his window back up again against any carried pong and watches for a while a small moth crawling quickly in loops across the dashboard and up on to the windscreen, small glittering flyer with folded wings scurrying frantically in 8-shapes. He attempts to catch it but it flutters away from his fingers several times so he crushes it with his thumb and regards the gold-flecked pasty smear on his skin, sniffs at it then wipes it off on his knee, rubs it in until it becomes indistinguishable from the innate shine of his shellsuit.

Darren gets back in the car, starts it.

—Good poo?

Darren shakes his head. —Fuckin squoze it out quick as I friggin well could, lar. Shits me up this place, tellin yeh. Member them fuckin murders up here, bout a year back?

—No.

—Yeh, it was in thee *Echo* an everythin. Darren six-point turns on the narrow lane and heads back up on to the main road. —Some local fuckin balloonhead wasted a few hikers. Don't remember it, no?

—Kind of. Was he the one with the gun?

—Gun? Nah, wasn't him. Don't know what he used

155

as a tool like, but I know it wasn't no gun. Got wellied by his mates or somethin, as I remember. Topped im, like.

He turns the car left, back on to the valley road overhung with a sky all one cloud cast-iron coloured. A distant lake doesn't gleam, just sits like smelt where the valley ends.

—Kept thinkin the cunt was gunner creep up on me when I was curlin one out, like.

—Who? The murderer? He's dead, inny?

—Someone else like him, well. Place's fuckin full of em, lar. Inbred fuckin maniacs bushwhackin people. Tellin yeh, Ally, place like this, thee wouldn't find yer body for fuckin months. Bet there's fuckin hundreds stashed away round here, on top of these friggin hills. In the lakes n stuff. Animals an birds'd friggin well eat yeh before yeh could be found. Probly some of the locals n all; nice bit o' boysteak tonight, Dai, look you!

Darren scratches at the swollen cleg bite on the back of his hand and Alastair smiles at the Welsh carica-ture accent and holds that smile as he looks out of the window up at the ever-wet colossal sawblades of the mountains and the valley ridges and the criss-crossing sheep tracks like capillaries and if he considers any element of the madness that has forever tumbled like scree off these severe slopes or of the violence that has fallen like the rain and lightning on them or of the raging blacknesses that must scorch themselves to ash in their eternal shadows then he gives no sign other than this small smile on his dry and peeling lips.

—Big fuckin hills around here, Ally, ey, says Darren but Alastair gives no sign of response and indeed in the gigantic world they pass through the only immediately readable sign is one man-made and blatant and weakly affixed into a patch of concrete at the valley's end like a twig, a child's toy, some small stick stuck in mud:

ABERYSTWYTH

20

PROMENADE

The four-sided shelter next to the bandstand is all cordoned off with police tape. Bright yellow tape snappin in the breeze an sayin: POLICE LINE DO NOT CROSS an triangular signs that say HEDDLU/STOPIWCH. What's gone on there, I wonder? Must be serious for it to be cordoned off. Suspicious, as well; a lot of people get snatched off the prom by big freak waves an that but there wouldn't be a bizzy presence for anythin like that, just a death by misadventure like, would there? So thee must be treatin it as iffy.

I go into the newsy's/general store on the prom by the courts to get some baccy. Nice lady works in here; always smiling, chatty.

—And how are you today then?

—Not bad, I say. —What's been goin on over the road?

—The police tape? Found the body of a young girl this morning, some jogger did. Only eighteen or so she was. Just sittin there on the bench, like, dead.

—Have thee any idea what from?

She shakes her head. —Maybe exposure, somethin like that. Had too much to drink and fell asleep and just died. Don't suppose they'll know for sure til the report comes out, the, erm, what's it called? That death report?

—Pathologist's report? Coroner's?

—That's it, coroner's report. Won't know for sure til then. Shock, tho, isn't it? Eighteen years old. What a waste. Makes you think, really, doesn't it?

—It does, aye.

—So sad.

—Yeh.

I buy me baccy an skins, put me bag of shoppin down to get the money out me pocket then pocket the tobacco an the change an pick the bag up again an say tara to the nice woman an leave the shop. So bright against the sea, that police tape. Luminous in the dark it is; this indication of suffering will blare yellow tonight in the windy salty dark. And another life gone. Unexpected, unanticipated, bevvied an tired an sit down for a wee bit an never fuckin wake up again. Everythin that's in a body, all thee entire worlds that're in a body cut up on some mortuary slab an then just nowt but compost. So fuckin close it is, that extinction. An closer to me than most others; I mean, part of me is already dead, literally, burnt in some hospital incinerator, part of me now just a smear of grease in the sky. Death an its decay I carry around with me in the space where me arm once was.

Went out to Strata Florida once, Ystrad Fflur like, them ancient abbey ruins. Dead peaceful, calm, lovely place, specially in the summer when all the flowers come out. So many bright colours. An in the grave-yard there's this one grave an all that's in it is a leg; some bloke, a sailor I think he was, had his leg chopped off an he buried it in the consecrated ground with full honours like, a big grand service, big funeral procession an everythin just for this one leg. Whether thee all thought it was a good laugh or thee were all deadly serious about it I don't know. Probly a bit of both. Got to have a sense of humour, like, when yer limbs start droppin off like leaves from trees or petals from a bunch of dandelions left in a glass of water on top of the TV. Can't be too fuckin ahl-arsed about it or you'll just go fuckin mad. It's only an *arm*, Christ. You've got another one, like.

Me arm

rot

aches with the weight of the shoppin

stinking pus-filled

an I auto

reeking leaking stench and decay

ME FUCKIN ARM ACHES WITH THE WEIGHT OF THE SHOPPING AND I AUTOmatically go to transfer it to me left hand before I remember that I don't have one. Them cells still working, still retaining their memory, still firing, like. It's social, the human cellular structure; each cell strivin to make some contact with thee other cells around it. Brain neurons makin connections with their neighbours or dyin through lack of contact. Through lack of stimulus. Strange, tho, how the cells that aren't there any more still seem to be doin their job, like, still seem to be sendin out messages. Ghost cells. Phantom cells still drifting through me empty sleeve.

I leave the shelter and its ring of doom-tape behind. The ring of tape so brightly coloured an what's the name for that? What's it called, when evolutionarily important messages are coveyed through colour? There's a word for it, isn't there? It's why we developed colour perception, so we could tell which fruits were ripe an ready to eat an which fungi an berries were poisonous. Like the police tape; the colour of it, as if it's warning me of danger. Don't come close, it says. Like them vivid caterpillars that no birds eat. There's a word for it. But I can't think what . . .

And there's no green in gangrene. Gangrene is fucking BLACK. Black as coal as seabed mud as cruelty as the fuckin grave

this bag of shopping's gettin dead, dead heavy. The handles have tightened into thin wires diggin into me palms an I imagine them snappin an all me shoppin spillin out an were that to happen then it just might be enough. Enough to send me into the nearest pub. I mean, yeh do all the hard fuckin work, yeh lay off the bevvy for weeks, months even, yeh use every last shred of yer will power to deny yerself somethin yer need an your reward is this, a snapped handle, a snapped shoelace, a big an unexpected bill. And you think: You fucking bastards. *This* is how yeh reward me, all my hard fuckin work. You purposely make bags an shoelaces weak so that we have to buy more, never mind the fuckin frustration that occurs in ar lives, thee embarrassment, so all ar hard work falls to shit an you send us back to the pub, *you* send us, an we're soon sleeping in garbage an it's all your fuckin fault, you faceless cunts behind desks, *this* is what you've made us do. Yeh just can't win. Think yer gettin things together, think yer sortin yerself out an the fuckin world throws *this* shit at you. Sick fuckin world. Sick fuckin

The handles hold an me shoulder aches with the weight of the bag an I quicken me pace towards the caff an a cold wind starts blowin spindrift in me face an makin me stump throb an again there's a couple of screamers on the bench by the burger booth, pisshead screamers bellowin gibberish, one in a bright orange filthy jacket. At one time I thought that shouted nonsense was the only valid response to the questions that the world chucks at you but now I know that that's rubbish. Self-defeatin rubbish. I mean, I've cleaned up, I've allowed me brain to rebuild itself, I've read some books an stared at the sky an the creatures that live in it an I know now how hollow that response is. Everything makes noises an those noises are important an it's only us, it seems, that count ar obsessions so valuable that we must scream them in the faces of others an there is absolutely no connection of any sort in this. It's a desperate an pathetic attempt *at* some kind of connection perhaps but it provokes nothing except a mass turning away an from the cellular level to the social level an all the levels in between, where there is no connection there is no life. Where there is no connection there is no fucking life. Only us and ar obsessions cos we're too fucking feeble to admit anything else.

Bag about to drop I barge in through the door of the caff an find a seat and let the bag go. Ahhhhhhh. Such a relief. Again on automatic I move what remains of me left arm up across me chest to massage me aching shoulder an then realise the futility an stop an move me right arm, me whole arm, in circles, pivoting it at the shoulder, flexing it, working out the muscle cramps. A waitress smiles at me an comes over with her pad.

—Iya.

—Just coffee please.

The T-shirt showing beneath her smock is yellow. The yellow of dandelions, wee-the-beds, Rebecca's favourite colour. Yellowyellowyellowyellow

—Cup or mug?

—Mug please. Great big one.

Ape-o. Apo. Ape-o seem.

—Iawn.

—An a piece of lemon cake as well.

—Iawn.

—Ta very much.

She goes off towards the back of the caff an I watch her arse move. Aposematic coloration, *that's* the fucking word.

Step 8: We made a list of all the persons we had harmed, and became willing to make amends to them all. And ignored the length of that list an thee enormity of those harms an thee utter impossibility of ever making true amends because to do so would involve invoking the saintly qualities of the human because such things very, very rarely exist and that fact we ignored also or rather conveniently forgot. And thee absences on that list gaped and howled ar mothers ar fathers ar own fucking limbs an in these white an blinding voids roared the questions an the prohibitions on their asking, why God creates us only to then go on an shatter us an why we are so swiftly turned to shells still living yet reeking an spent and otiose from upright to blemish in one heartbeat, one mere circuit of ar polluted blood. Our propensity to build lists, ar propensity just to LIST, tabulate the forces that wreck us incrementally. How fatuous it all seems.

CAR

—Darren, can yeh not stop wrigglin around in yer seat? Yer swervin us all over the friggin road, man.

—Yeh, well, I'm tryna scratch me fuckin cleft, aren't I? Couldn't wipe proper like, so it's itchy as fuck.

He takes one hand off the wheel and reaches down under his arse and rummages and sighs. —That's berrer. Shifted a few clinkers. It's that fuckin Manchester's fault; can't even be a decent arsewipe like, knowmean?

An old town approaching over the old stone bridge that spans the brown and swollen river. This neo-capital over the water under a low sky damply a-brew, terraces whitewashed or left in the original granite and blue-stone and a few spikes of spires, clock tower projecting its dial above it all except the shadowing mountain cloud-capped and from that cloud a vast misty lace descending to obscure its fourth face. Glyndŵr's supposed parliament buildings, one brown barn hidden by the gawping sightseers, and the bunting and the flags and the declamatory signposts pointing towards itself and also Celtica and also the mound where the unification ceremony was held where Glyndŵr levitated and wars were worked out into not-war except towards one common enemy and that mound now just a sodden mudded hump, one lone figure in

Gore-tex making notes on a damp pad. Alastair observes this solitary figure as they pass.

—Mack-in-leth, Darren murmurs. —How djer pronounce this place, Ally? Them two els, like, thee don't make an el sound, do thee? More of a kay, innit? Mack-in-*keth*. Like that, yeh?

—Nah, it's more of a kay *el*. Like in 'clean' or summin.

—Mach-in-*kleth*.

—Summin like that, yeh.

They approach a railway bridge. Bilingual flood-warning sign but there is no flood and another road sign which Darren nods at.

—I mean, look at this fuckin language, lar. It's fuckin *well* mad. 'Araf', now what the fuck does 'araf' mean? How the fuck am I supposed to know what fuckin 'araf' means?

—It means 'slow'. Look, it says underneath: 'slow'. It's in English as well, yeh dozy get.

—Yer arse.

They pass under the railway bridge through a puddle of river water that has collected there, four tan fans thrown by the wheels, and enter the small town proper. Bus station and pubs on the right and a terrace on the left and ahead set in an elevated square of cobbles the war memorial sporting a fresh wreath although today is no commemoration of calendrically recognised significance. Just one old lady from this clutch of houses and her sixty-year-old bad news still raw. Alastair looks out at the passing town, the stone and wood and slate of the buildings seeping as if perpetually wet, an archipelago of green horseshit around the memorial sprouting tufts of undigested straw but no horse or rider to be seen, as if the past and its emblems excremental or otherwise will intrude or will not be concreted over, built on, not entirely, no. Alastair gazes through glass at glass and the surrounding steelwork of the window-housing and there may be some fancy in him that those reflective surfaces have stored in them something gone and forgotten chain-mail perhaps and mane and that on certain days when the light is right and ozone crackles in the air about to split and storm they may offer to him precisely that. Shadows of such times.

It is market day; a long line of traffic at the lights on red, cars and trucks and drays. A road branches off, lined with stalls tarpaulin-covered red-and-white-striped canvas and offerings of fruit and vegetables, cheap clothes, meat, cheese, trinkets. Three hundred people down that road stall-dawdling and drifting. Darren joins the queue of vehicles and hisses impatient through his teeth and stares at some teenagers sitting blankly in the shelter of the clock tower but they stare straight through him, do not see him, appear in fact to see nothing at all.

—Aw, fer fuck's sakes. Gunner be all fuckin day at this rate.

—It's alright, Da. Not far now.

—You've been sayin that for the last two fuckin hours, yeh cunt.

—No I haven't.

—Yes yeh fuckin av.

—Well, it *isn't* very far now. Honest. Bout twenny mile. Be there in thirty.

—What time is it now?

Alastair looks up at the clock tower. —Three bells nearly. Plenty of time, lar.

—Won't be unless these friggin lights change an these cunts gerrer fuckin move on. Been drivin all fuckin day.

—I'd take over only –

—Yeh, yeh, I know, only yeh lost yer friggin licence. So yeh keep sayin. Soft cunt drivin while pissed up, you. Count yerself lucky yeh didn't get banged up.

—I did.

—Did yeh?

—Aye, yeh.

—Where?

—Walton. Did thirty days. Piecer fuckin piss, mate. Tellin yeh.

—Yeh, but now yeh can't fuckin drive, can yeh? It's not the time, lar, it's the fuckin, thee inconvenience. The not bein fuckin mobile, like.

—Doesn't bother me. Still get behind the wheel, like, doan I?

—Yeh, well, yer not goin to today. Tommy'd fuckin gut us wither carvin knife if this one goes cunt up, knowmean? No fuckin messin.

Red changes to green and the traffic moves, most vehicles veering left into the market and the remainder heading directly onwards over the roundabout towards the coast and it is this thin stream that Darren joins, a yellow open-topped MG in front of him and a camper van behind him, an escort of holidaymakers moving slowly out of the town. Darren chugs past a bus stop on which is advertised a book called something like

The Boss, some autobiography of some underworld figure and a large image of that figure's face choice-bald and snarling in a purple tint.

—Aw, fuckin ell, Ally, look at that, will yis? Darren points and Alastair looks. —Another fuckin *buke* by some no-mark fuckin balloonhead goin on about his useless fuckin life. Probly spent most of it in fuckin jail n all, soft cunt couldn't stop gettin caught. Who reads this fuckin shit, lar? Who *buys* that fuckin shite?

Traffic accelerates and Darren does too. The MG quickly vanishes. Alastair shrugs.

—It's all the bleedin posh twats, innit? Yeh know how fuckin beaky thee are. University teachers an arseholes like that, thee all get off on all that kinda stuff.

Darren nods. —Is right, lar, yeh. Fuckin wankmags for them people, them fuckin bukes are. Wanner read about how the scum live, like. Only way thee get some fuckin excitement in their lives, innit? Get their fuckin kicks, like, readin about how some fat southern ponce stabbed some cunt or glassed some cunt. Pure fuckin arseholes them bastards, tellin yeh.

—Is right. Alastair smiles. —Ey, imagine if Tommy wrote one. Imagine wharrit'd be like.

Darren laughs and affects a brain-dead, toneless voice. —Hello-my-name-is-Tommy-Maguire-an-I-am-a-gangster. I-av-a-great-big-belly-an-a-perm.

Alastair takes it up. —I-like-bein-a-gangster-it-is-dead-great. People-are-all-scared-of-me-an-I-like-to-hit-people-I-do.

—No-ladies-fancy-me-cos-I-am-so-ugly-so-I-have-to-pay-ladies-to-suck-my-knob. My-knob-is-

tiny-an-I-have-a-giant-sweaty-smelly-bumcrack-an-
it-hangs-out-of-my-kex.

They laugh. Alastair continues. —Bein-a-gangster-
is-my —

—Alright, Ally, enough now, eh? Don't tear the
friggin arse out of it, lad. Do somethin useful with
yerself an light us up a ciggie.

Alastair does and they sit there smoking as the landscape around them flattens into a huge bog spread to
distant dunes on their right, sparkle of sea beyond that
and a pale blue ridge of mountains. Alastair sniggers.

—What's so fuckin funny?

—That.

—What?

—All that stuff about Tommy. Makes me laugh, like.

Small smile from Darren. —Aye, twat'd need a whole
fuckin *crew* of ghost writers, wouldn't he?

—Ghost writers? What the fuck's a ghost writer?

—Yeh don't know what a ghost writer is?

—Wouldn't be askin if I did, would I?

—Don't get lippy, Ally. Simple fuckin yes or no
would've done.

—What is one, well?

—A ghost writer is someone who writes someone
else's buke for them. Which most of them fuckin
celebrity gangsters have cos they're all stupid thick
cunts, like. Can't fuckin read or write, most of em.
Shit-fer-brains, like. Soft in thee ed. Tell yeh what,
tho . . . Darren's face clouds. —Bet they're all fuckin
brewstered.

—Yeh reckon?

—Oh aye, yeh. Get a friggin wad for them fuckin

bukes, tellin yeh. An some other twat writes em. Do fuck all an get a fuckin *wad*. Bastards.

—An here's us workin for friggin buttons. Not on, lar, is it?

Darren does not respond or if he does Alastair does not hear him. Both of them set-faced staring out at the road reeled in by the trundling axles or slurped up by the bonnet.

And Darren: camera flash around his face that face on TV expensive suit the cocky clever way he would answer the questions, in some huge hotel holding court in the bar wood-panelled and a mound of paper money on his bed and the women the women the women. I'm just a poor lad from Toxteth, Graham. Working-class boy done good. Only ever hurt me own yeh I *would* say there's a kind of honour in it a nobility even yeh an now here's my just reward moneywomen-recognition at last some achievement fuck yes.

And Alastair: storm-battered castle wind wailing and him in a colossal hall bent over a huge wooden desk old and chipped writing by candlelight with a quill pen and the flame flickers and at the edge of the cast light in the black shadows there a misty grey shape behind him, over his shoulder, some vapour vaguely human, dry-leaf voice whispering in his ear the wondrous words and sentences he faithfully records on to the yellow vellum page.

A sign reads:

ABERYSTWYTH

12

CAFF

Never used to go into caffs, me. It was always pubs with me. Only ever drank tea or coffee or milk or whatever when I'd just got out of bed unless I was on a big, *bad* bender an then it'd be whisky for brekkie. Beer. Vodka n flat Coke. Boakin up yellow bile in the bowl at the side of the bed an then that first drink necked in one an the gaggin an the heavin the pure fuckin struggle to keep the stuff down. An if yeh could, if yeh could keep it down in yer stomach, then yeh *knew* that yer'd be alright. That everythin was gunner be fine that day. No spew blood-streaked on yer chin or in the bog, just that settling inside you as the bevvy did its magic, its lovely, lovely work but the spew tho the puke just remember the dribblin sick.

An the piss.

But caffs, tho, thee just never figured on me mental radar. I just never went into them, thee had nothing to offer me. Caught in a downpour? Nip into an alehouse. Or stay in the one yer already in. Need a wee sit-down? Duck into a pub. Caffs were always something that other people did, like work or wash the car or visit garden centres. Part of a world removed from me. If I ever got hungry I'd have a sweaty cheese roll from the placcy box behind the bar or a toastie wrapped in a paper towel or just a bag of crisps or nuts with the next drink. Caffs just never offered me anythin I wanted. Old ladies would go into caffs. They were designed for ahl dears to have a sit an a gab or for students to sit an fret about their friggin essays or for pretentious posing ponces to read books over espressos. Which are other things that never featured in me life; books. Waste of fuckin time, I thought. Didn't have time to read, I had me *own* thoughts to work out, an anyway reading ate into valuable drinkin time. I do read *now*, tho, oh yeh. One of the first things I took up when the boredom of sobriety began to set in. You can beat that, with books. You can reopen the world, with books. You can

tingle

then

A prickling in me arms, includin the one that isn't there. Unpleasant deep prickling in me skin. Heart beginning to thump. Everythin rapidly takin on an unreal sheen all threatening an nightmarish that waitress has evil lying eyes and thee old women are whispering about me none of this seems real as if I am a guest unwelcome in someone else's fevered dream terror lies under the coffee cup a thin frail veneer beyond which lies shit and horror I can hear my heartbeat hear my breath it is another

panic attack panic attack fuckin fuckin panic attack

feel compelled to move altho what that would solve I do not know hysteria in me teeth just GET THE FUCK OUT OF HERE

feel like this will never pass but it

will

pass

these such horrible fuckin things thee come so without warning. The tingling skin an then

Oh Christ I've got to get away from here

there is something very fuckin bad comin for me pure evil on its way to shatter me

gunner be sick cannot breathe heart like a fuckin machine gun my fingers shaking my stump screaming rapidly swallowing a terror on me in my skull feel like I've eaten maggots an they're writhing an squirming down in there the room spinning all evil on its way already here the entire world is sinister an pure fuckin hates me

I turn me head to look behind me at the sea as if there's any solace to be found there and see a sparrow hopping along the pavement common little brown house sparrow hops a few times pecks somethin off the paving slab some tiny mite or ant or something an flies away I watch it fly

and most familiar of British birds wherever there are people there will be this little bird altho population declining rapidly for reasons unknown probably predator increase domestic cat culpable. Male: streaked brown and black above, grey crown and chocolate nape with black bib across breast. Female: brown with striped back grey underbelly lacks bib but has prominent pale eyebrow and double wingbar. Gregarious, nests in houses bushes trees wherever suitable which is most places. Colonial behaviour flitting flight eats seeds and insects an bread an one time hung-over in Williamson Square I fed one a crisp straight out of me hand

can't remember what flavour probly salt n vinegar

cos that was thee only thing me alcohol-strafed taste buds could register but I do remember thee occasion; waiting for Rebecca to cash her giro or was it to trade something in at Cash Converters so we could drink more so I could shred my head so I could sit in a caff some years later in a Welsh seaside town an have another fucking

panic attack

I AM HATED

attacked by panic ah fuck sweating now breathing heavily be calm be still it is starting to pass the sparrow is gone but there is a

black an vicious evil shape on its way

no there is a

vileness inside everything

no there is a

sickness in human life

no there is a

crow hopping up the slipway from the beach to peck at a scrunched-up chip wrapper, altho not really hopping crows tend to walk not hop a kind of rolling-shouldered swagger beak like a black blade

this fucking

fear

fear in my skin

carrion crow: large and familiar all-black bird with heavy bill and aggressive habits. More robustly built than other similar species like the rook and the jackdaw and the hooded crow and more isolated except in winter months when may form colonies to amass at rich food sources such as landfills. Generally a scavenger but will take baby birds or the eggs of other birds or insects and worms or the eyes and anuses of newborn lambs leading to poisoning and shooting by farmers. Subspecies hooded crow has grey back belly and rump habituates towns and heaths and estuaries and woods and hedges almost everywhere in fact and its voice is a loud shrill cry

a scream

and when it flies like it does now its primaries spread like fingers and through them gush light. How? I mean, there's no sun in that flat grey sky but the bird spreads his wings an light seems to fall

I think

I think maybe

it's gone. I think maybe

I'm calm again. Thee ahl ladies are just talkin about traffic congestion in the town ('DuwDuw. Shockin. Isn't it terrible?') an the waitress is just butterin bread an hummin along to the Samantha Mumba song on the radio an that's all that's goin on.

It's all okay. I think I'm calm again.

evil/no

I finish me coffee. Sit starin into thee empty cup, the froth on the bottom a silhouette of Abraham Lincoln's head. Is that right? Is that observation permissible? I mean, it's not sinister or insane or anything to have a thought like that? Nah; it's just an observation, that's all it is. Me heartbeat stays calm, me skin doesn't prickle, me breathing is steady an normal. It's just an observation. An anyway, he friggin well *did* resemble froth with that mad bleedin beard.

Fuckin panic attacks. Legacy of the wreckage wrought by booze. Alcohol fuckin psychosis – it still lingers. It'll never go away. Once an alky always a fuckin alky but there are medicines:

Diazepam, 2–5mg for short-term treatment. A downer, like. Or beta blockers to relieve palpitations an the physical symptoms such as breathlessness, rapid racing heartbeat, shaking limbs, fear, dizziness. Or for longer-term treatment: tricyclic antidepressants like imipramine.

Or: as one of thee ahl hippies in the clinic used to say, panic attacks are caused by a disturbance of chitta (thee organ of perception and cognition) and are, in ayurvedic medicine, referred to as chitta udvega. The disturbance unbalances the vata energy which then causes trembling, fear, dizziness, etc. As a cure there is the marma-point head massage with Jyotishmatic oil and abhyanga, using vata-balancing ashwagandha-brahmic oil. Or the herbal wine, Sarasvatarishtha, which helps relieve pain. Too hung up on Western chemicals, man, as thee ahl wrecked hippie would say. Free your soul . . . said the man who'd banged up so much smack his fuckin arms looked like Twiglets.

Or: fuck it all it's all just shite panic an pain are conditions of existence in this shitty world an this shitty life if we didn't panic we'd be dead. Just another thing to conquer, panic attacks are, another horror to overcome an fuckin overcome them I will. Me an the crows an the sparrows will beat them to a pulp. Drag em down an alley an give em a good fuckin kickin.

Right, now I'm hungry. Bleedin starvin, in fact. An loads to do back at home; unpack me shoppin, check on Charlie an give im some celery and a pat, pick some vedge for me tea then cook me tea then eat me tea. Then have a bath an watch some telly. Maybe give Perry a bell, get him round for a game of cards or somethin. An all this to be done with only one fuckin arm. Takes twice as long.

Try an deal for a game of rummy with only one hand an you'll see how fuckin long it takes. Try holdin yer cards. Try fuckin *shufflin* em.

But I can fuckin do it, tho. I'm still alive. *Nothin* beats me, *nothin* lays me low.

I leave money for the coffee on the table an say tara to the waitress an take up me shoppin bag an leave. Still a black sky, but the threatened rain hasn't arrived yet. Good. If it stays off until I get home, then everything's gunner be sound; the rest of me life's gunner be perfectly okay.

Step 9: We made direct amends to such people wherever possible, except when to do so would injure them or others. Yeh, we took ar shivering selves, ar bleating sacks of bodies missing teeth an eyes an even fuckin limbs an a certain spark or glint or whatever it is we once had an we said in voices of tumbling ashes that we were willing to make redress. And the reflections wept or laughed or both an thee empty sky just grumbled an we knew, then, that any reparation was so terribly remote an that we must drift through guilt an rue an sorrow for ever. Banished to some starless shore backlit all red and utterly alone there for ever, us arselves an everyone we'd ever touched, to wander pointlessly for ever. All these for evers. All these insane ultimates.

CAR

Darren is singing tunelessly a Bloodhound Gang song:

—You an me baby ain't nothin but mammals, so let's do it like thee do on the Discovery Channel, doorigginnow. You an me baby ain't nothin but mammals, so let's do it like thee do on the Discovery Channel, dooriggin now. You an me baby . . .

The same line over and over. It's getting on Alastair's wick. He points to a road sign that tells them that their destination is only seven miles away and says in a kind of Uncle Tom voice: —Nearly der, massa. Wahl, tank de Lawd fo' dat.

This stops Darren singing. —What yeh talkin like that for?

—Like what?

—Like some friggin Yardie or somethin?

—I wasn't, I was just, yer know . . . avin a mess, like, that's all.

—Yeh, well. Don't fuckin talk to me about fuckin Yardies, lar.

—I wasn't.

—Yeh, well, don't, that's all. Did yeh hear that story? About the hands, like?

—No.

—Only a couple a weeks ago it was. Yeh know that feller Flathead?

—Is that the dead skinny bloke with the flat head?

—That's the one, aye. He's got –

—I flogged him a bike.

—Eh?

—That Flathead, I flogged him a bike. Fifty notes, mountain bike, like. *Was* me uncle's but he had to get rid of it when his rectum prolapsed, like, so he gave it to me an I flogged it on.

—Fifty nicker?

—Aye, yeh.

—Not bad.

—I know, yeh. Cost me fuck all as well.

—Well, anyway, this Flathead's got a little brother, bout sixteen or somethin, works as a cycle courier. Bout two weeks ago he gets called to –

—Probly uses that same bike. See, it –

—Will yeh just shut the fuck up an listen to wharram sayin? Fuck's sakes, Alastair, yer like a friggin *gnat* in me fuckin ear. Whinin on. Just shut the fuck up an let me tell yis this story, will yeh? Might even fuckin learn summin.

Alastair shrugs and sniffs and shuts up. Darren stares at him for a beat of three then refaces front and continues.

—Flathead's little brother. Cycle courier on this bike that was maybe yer uncle's til his arse fell out an he passed it on to you an you flogged it on. That better?

Alastair nods and grins. —Yeh.

—Good. So he gets called to an address down Parly, by Somali Town, yeh know it? So he goes there, knocks on the door, ten-foot friggin Yardie guy comes out an

179

gives im a metal box, like, freezin fuckin cold as if it's been in the fuckin fridge or summin, an a wad as big as his fist. Doesn't say a word, like, just gives him the box an the swag an a piece of paper with an address on it somewhere down the Dock Road by the Dingle. Flathead's bro pockets the cash, like, puts the box in his bag an sets off.

Darren picks something out of his teeth and flicks it on to the floor.

—Anyway, he's halfway down the Dock Road like, an he hears a rattlin. Comin from his bag, like, this loud rattlin sound. So he stops his bike, gets off, looks in the bag. The metal box had burst open. So he takes a peek inside. I mean, yeh would, wouldn't yeh?

—Oh aye, yeh.

—Guess what he sees.

—Norrer scooby.

—A pairer fuckin hands. Hacked off, like. Still with the rings on an evrythin. He said that one of em had a tat of a swallow an there was five or six fuckin sovs left on em.

Darren takes a hand off the steering wheel to display his own sovereign rings.

—Jesus Christ. Straight up, this?

Darren nods firm. —No fuckin lie, lar. Pairer fuckin hands.

—Fuck. Alastair shakes his head, his eyes wide. —What did he do, Flathead's little brother?

—What the fuck djer *think* he did? He delivered the fuckin box. Went to thee address, like, handed it over to another big Yardie who looks in it like an says:

It is done. Just that, like, yer know in one a them big deep voices? IT IS DONE. Gives the kid another stack of cash like an closes the friggin door.

—Jesus fuckin Christ.

—Is right, man. I saw him, Flathead's brother, two or three days later, in the Dart. He'd been on one forty-eight hours. White as a sheet, looked like he'd seen a fuckin ghost.

—I'm not friggin surprised. Poor little get. One thing, tho; were thee black or white?

—What?

—Them hands. Were thee a black feller's or a white feller's?

—Dunno. Does it matter, like?

—Suppose not, no. Hands is hands, aren't thee?

—Is right. Tell yeh what, tho; it's a good fuckin way of doin business. Ruthless, like, that's the way yer've gorrer be. No fuckin messin around. If fuckin Tommy was a bit more friggin business-minded, like, we wouldn't be on this stupid fuckin shitty little job, would we?

Alastair looks out at the fields on either side spreading dull green in the grey light to far hills beginning now to speckle with scattered houses, outskirts of council estates like odd forests. A tall TV mast like some thin kingbuilding and a column on a tall far hill, probable monument to some gone war. He says:

—Not far, now. Nearly there. Another few minutes, that's all.

—Well, thank fuck for that. Get the fuckin thing sorted an fuck off home.

Alastair smiles. —Tell yeh what, tho; the bloke who

had his hands chopped off. He *would* need a friggin ghost writer, wouldn't he?

—Oh yeh. Darren laughs. —Deffo.

—Is he dead, djer think?

—God, yeh. Loss of blood, like, an the shock. He'll be brown fuckin bread like this daft cunt *sheep*!

Stray sheep at road side and Darren swerves suddenly at it an it darts into the hedge, hindquarters missed by inches.

—Missed the fucker.

—Good fuckin job n all, Da. Put a great big fuckin dent in Tommy's car that would've.

—Oo fuck, yeh. Never thought about tha. That fuckin *would* be all, woulden it?

—Is right. Have to do a runner, hide out in these friggin hills, like.

—Nah. He'd find us. Reckons he knows this area, like, says he's made one or two fuckin graves out here. Gobshite that he is.

—Who? Tommy?

—Yeh. The gobshite. Graves me arse; I mean, fat cunt Tommy climbin these mountains cartin a body an a spade? No fuckin way, man. Cunt starts fuckin wheezin when he climbs the friggin stairs. I've seen him.

—Yeh, but knowin him, he'd just get others to do it. Get the suckholes like Jez Sully an his creepin fuckin mates to do the dirty work for im. Never does it isself, does he?

—You *know* it, Ally. Zackly what *we're* fuckin doin, innit?

—Is right. The people he was gunner bump, he'd

gerrem to dig their own graves first, like. Like thee always do in the films.

Darren's brow wrinkles. A deep V forms in the skin at the bridge of his nose between his eyes.

—Yeh, never fuckin understood that, me. That diggin-yer-own-grave stuff. I mean, gunner friggin die anyway, I'd tell em to do it themfuckinselves. If thee do, then yer've gorrer chance of leggin it or battlin em, an if thee don't, then they're stuck there with a dead body an no grave. Yeh can't lose.

—Sept yer'd be dead.

—Yeh, but thee were gunner kill yeh anyway, weren't thee? Dig yer own grave, fucks. I'd say do it yerfuckin-self. Cunt. Not gunner help youse out in gettin rid of me own fuckin corpse, fuck that. Sack that shit, lar. I'd tell em to do it their fuckin self.

But just the heart beating for ten more minutes just ten more minutes of breath, bloodthud. Just the world through your eyes for ten more minutes even if that world has been shrunk to a patch of churned earth and a figure behind and above you with a gun aimed at your skull. What you might think in those ten minutes. How you could live like you've never lived before in those final ten minutes the culmination majestic and magnificent of all that you could possibly be in those closing minutes and the fury with which you'd dig turned pure as if to flee in the only direction possible from the surface threat and terror above, down down and further down through soil and rock to that harrowed fuming blazing heart that absorbs you and is not alien is known to you because its issue has turmoiled and tumulted through you for so much red and frenzied time.

Darren looks out at the passing pinewoods on his right, the dense shadows between the trees. Murmurs:

—Not a bad place for the job, out here. Privacy, like.

—What?

—Them woods. Plenty of privacy like, to do this one-armed get.

—What, bring im out here?

—Aye, yeh. Stick im in the fuckin boot. Tell im to dig his own grave, see if he'll do it.

—He's only got one arm.

—So?

—So how's he gunner be able to dig?

—Can use a fuckin trowel, can't he? Get him to dig with a fuckin trowel, like.

—Take ages.

—So? You in some kinda big rush, are yeh?

—I can't waste anyone, Darren.

—So yeh keep sayin.

—No, I mean it; I just can't.

—No one's fuckin *askin* yer to. We're just gunner shit the fucker up, that's all. Just gunner say boo. Birrer fear, birruva welly, that's all. No one said anythin about slaughterin, did thee?

Alastair just shrugs.

—An anyway, Ally, answer me this: if yeh were lost out in these mountains, like, starvin, freezin, could yeh kill someone then?

—What for?

—To eat, softlad. I mean, could yeh kill an eat someone if yer life depended on it?

—What, out here?

—Yeh.

—No. I mean, we're only a few miles from a town. There'll be a supermarket there an evrythin.

—No, I don't fuckin mean right exactly *here*, soft-arse, I mean, yer know. In a wilderness, like. No food or anythin. If there was a choice of dyin or turnin into a cannibal, what would yeh do?

—Dunno, really. Depends on who I was with. Wouldn't eat Tommy.

—Why not? Could live off that fat twat for years.

—Yeh, but it'd be all fat. All slobbery jelly, like, ick.

—*I* friggin well could. I mean, stayin alive, like, that's thee only thing. Eat any fucker to stay alive, me. Tellin yeh.

The road rises. They pass under a railway bridge with SAEFON ALLAN painted on it and the rise becomes steeper and they are heading into the waxy sky.

—Wharrabout if yeh were stuck in a desert an there was no water. Would yeh drink yer own piss?

Darren shakes his head. —Trust fuckin *you* to think about that, Alastair. Piss-drinkin. An I know *you* would; in fact, you'd probly start drinkin yer own slash before the fuckin water run out. Like one a them German cunts in Eddie's films, you.

—Already have done.

—Ey?

—Drank piss, like. When I was a kid. Someone bet me that I wouldn't drink a cup of me own wee like, so I did. Just like salty water.

—Yeh dirty get.

185

—Just like sea water. An it was me *own*, like, I mean, I wouldn't go anywhere fuckin *near* anybody else's. An I got ten fags out of it. He shrugs. —No big deal. I'd do it again if I was skint.

—Yeh dirty frigger. It's fuckin poison, lar.

—Poison? So's all that fuckin bugle an billy yeh stick up yer snipe. Don't see yis worryin about *that*.

Darren grins. —That's cos it feels fuckin top. An wharrabout you, ey? Mister human fuckin Hoover there? Surprised yer've got any friggin snipe left, you. Surprised yer not like tha *EastEnders* one, djer know the one I mean?

Alastair does not answer this question, distracted as he is by the scratting chickens in the small market garden they pass, the mud-and-gravel drive on to the road in which two hens and a rooster peck and scurry. One flutters for a few metres frantic and clucking away from the car and Alastair laughs.

—Look at the chickens, Da! Look at em go! G'wahn, lads, give it some welly!

Darren snorts. —Be eatin one a them, you will, next time yer pissed up an fancy some fried wings, yeh cunt. Might be one a them exact same ones, yeh snidey bastard.

—No way. Alastair shakes his head all serious. —Never gunner eat fried chicken again, man.

—Go way. You fuckin *love* the stuff, you. Seen yis eat a whole fuckin bucket of it, yeh lyin get.

—Not lyin, man, just not gunner ever eat it again, that's all.

—Why? Yer not gunner tell me yer've gone fuckin vedgie. Not *you*.

—No, just not gunner eat fried chicken again. Simple as.

—Why not, like? Must be a reason.

—Yeh, well, yeh know me sister? The one that lives down in London now?

—The one with the tits? Aw *yeh*. Fuck her stupid, I would, lar, no lie.

—She's me *sister*.

—I know, yeh. Amazin innit that you're so butt-ugly an she's worth doin. What's she gorrer do with chickens, anyway?

—Well, she was up in town last week like, an we went out on thee ale an we're down Hardman Street an she wants some scran. Gets a chicken burger, like, asks for no mayo cos she gets eczema or somethin an she comes out all scabby if she eats it. Bites into it outside like, an it tastes like shite an a load of white gooey stuff squirts out. She goes back in, says she asked for no mayo, guy in the place says he didn't put any on. So she looks inside, like, lifts the lid of the roll off an guess wharrit fuckin was?

—Aw no.

Alastair nods. —Aye, yeh. Only a great big fuckin cyst, like, wannit? That's what the white gooey shite was – pus. Believe that, lar?

—Fuck's sakes. That is pure sick. Pure fuckin *hangin*, that, man.

—Innit? So no more fried chicken for me, lar. Never again in me fuckin life.

—Is right. Fuckin pusburgers. Cyst-in-a-bun. Fuck *that*.

The hill begins to level. Long hill this, gradual

climb such height above the sea. The crest nears.

—That's got me thinkin, tho, Ally.

—What has?

—Yer sister, like. White stuff dribblin out of her gob. Next time she's up from London let me know an it won't be chicken pus, I'll tell yeh that.

—She's me bleedin *sister*, Darren.

—I know, yeh. Can ardly fuckin believe it meself. Tell me she's adopted.

Darren laughs and Alastair says nothing and they reach the hill's level crest a brief plateau before re-descent and the houses now crowd to the road's edges and big university buildings appear, slices of red brick and unreflective glass behind fences and a few trees. Metropolis this seems after the miles and hours of sparse villages and mountains and valleys empty of human habitation this abrupt town at land's end and the road starts to slope and the town proper is laid out far below them, horizontal honeycomb of grey and brown and off-white flat between two huge hills and larger buildings of hospital and college rising above the terraces and streets like whales among a smaller shoal or as if those same whales had hauled themselves on to land from the sea beyond against which what meek missile of light the dull sun has launched along the valley from miles distant now detonates in an airburst of ethereal glitterings, a soft blast of brass shrapnel that hangs over the unexpected settlement.

Alastair: —Bigger than I thought it'd be.

Darren: —Just fuckin made up we're here. Here we go; keep yer eyes peeled for a one-armed thievin cunt who jacks little kids.

—Alright.

They drive down the hill, into the town, as if seeking the sea. A sign reads:

ABERYSTWYTH
CROESO

CASTLE

This bag of shoppin's so friggin heavy it's pullin me
down, makin me shoulder burn with muscle fatigue
an I'm gettin knackered. Gunner have a right arm like
Lennox friggin Lewis, I am, with all the work it has
to do unaided; never gets to rest, me right arm, unless
I'm sleepin, like. Always on the go, it is. Relentless
strain on it. Should get meself one a them wee trolleys
like thee ahl biddies have; that'd make things easier.
Just stick me shoppin in it an pull it along behind me.
Probly look dead daft, like, but fuck that. I've only got
one arm.

Or some kind of robot case. A cart or somethin that
yeh can put yer shoppin in an it'll be programmed to
follow yeh wherever yeh go like a faithful little dog.
Just trundlin along behind yis followin yeh home or
wharrever or waitin patiently for yeh outside the caff
or the pub oh no not the pub just the caff. Pure brill-
iant, that would be, a robot shoppin trolley. Must be
easy to make, as well, I mean, I'm sure there wouldn't
be much to it. Thee can put guidance systems in cruise
fuckin missiles, can't thee? So why not shoppin trolleys?
They'd even be able to get back out of the ponds n
rivers that pissed-up idiot students chuck em into of
a Saturday night. Imagine the scene of a Sunday
mornin, all the trolleys drippin wet an draped in weed

creakin slowly along the streets an across the parks, all of em headed back home to Somerfield car park, convergin on that big cavernous building as if on friggin Mecca or summin. All them trundlin trolley-bots.

Pick up the pace, now. Gerrer fuckin move on. Belly's rumblin with hunger an me right shoulder's complaining, gettin louder with each step. Plus the sky's gone even blacker an looks like it's gunner split at any time an I really don't wanner get drenched an catch a cold. Had one last winter, pure fuckin horrible it was – tryin to make meself comfortable with a cold an only one arm. Tryin to make soup wrapped in a duvet which keeps slippin off yeh cos yeh can't hold it tight to yer body an stir a pan of leek an potato at the same time. Shiverin, sweatin, mounds of bogey-crusted tissues all around yeh. Pure fuckin horrible. An me arm hadn't long come off then so I was still gettin used to it an the whole winter or most of it was vile. An I wanner avoid repeatin it, if at all possible.

So quick fuckin home, through the castle. Get a friggin move on now.

I pass round the crazy-golf course an through the noisy gulls clustered around the old lady who feeds them breadcrumbs at this spot at this time every single day an enter the castle at what must've been the inner moat, now tarmacked over, at its bottom, like, what would've been the moat-bed. It's like a wee valley now, a smaller model of the much much larger one the castle an thee entire town are built in. A few kids with faces like cottage cheese are standin under the drawbridge; I see one a them hide a canister of lighter fluid up his baggy sleeve as I pass. He's dead, dead spotty; cottage cheese with chives, then. Just discoverin all the joys of intoxicated escape, thee are, about fifteen, sixteen years old. Just gettin to know wharrit's like when all the world opens up before you as you fall out of it. An it must seem to them now that this world is stuffed full of possibilities but the probability is this, here, *me*, a one-armed tremblin shadow scurryin home alone through a ruined castle in a town he's not from, humpin a bag of shoppin carefully chosen to feed only himself, just one person an his pet rabbit. An thee empty sleeve flappin. Look at it, children, this is what awaits. But I still wish I was you; all them years ahead of youse, them mad fuckin years ahead, all that time for runnin an roarin an bein

SO FUCKING ALIVE

before *this* shit happens to youse. Enjoy it while yeh can. It won't last long. But it'll seem like several fuckin fiery lifetimes while it goes on.

I walk quickly up out of the moat an through the tower from which some Brummie tourist fell an died a month or two back an across thee inner what? Sanctum? Field? Thee inner grassy bit. Through the circle of standin stones altho they're not the real thing, like, thee were planted only a few decades ago to add, I suppose, a wee bit of Celtic mystery as if this needed adding to, this castle sacked several times over which changed hands again n again among a sea of blood and Glyndŵr holding it against cannon an hordes an hurricanes of steel an stone an flame. All these stones here, black blood at the core of each an every one. Hard sponges, like, soakin up all that spilled blood. An the sea itself, dark an moody, an the mountainous coastline in each direction, north an south the sharp cliffs rising high an buckled out of the haze an the mist, as *if* all this needed any adulteration. As if it could ever be augmented in its enigma by anything, especially these tacky granite blocks like coffins upright, now sprayed an chipped by graffiti, words from a paint tin or bolster. But they're good for one thing at least cos I duck down to hide behind one as I see Phil, that smelly lad with the bad stutter stridin all hurried past the war memorial. He looks like a man on a mission, skinny an scruffy but determined, an I hide behind a stone cos I don't want him to see me cos

a) his stutter's so bad he'll take ten minutes to say hello an I'm hungry an tired an wanner be home, an

b) the mission he appears to be on will no doubt involve a shitload of drugs and/or drink an it's best for me to remain as far from temptation as I possibly can, an

c) he has a tendency to pong a bit. Honest to God; he niffs. The fucker *reeks*.

I watch him circle the war memorial then cringe as one a them fuckin jets screams over dead low, so sudden them fuckers, I mean yeh can't even hear the noise of them until they're on top of yeh, like, an splittin the sky, shriekin so fuckin loud yer ears twang an yer heart races an yer skull starts pounding. It roars over the memorial an the statue on top of it, the bint holdin thee olive wreath (ho fuckin ho) an Phil watches it for a moment as it banks n shrinks in the sky further down the coast an the screech diminishes, just remains as a pulse in thee air then he scurries down thee embankment an on to the prom. A car, an old green Moggy Minor, stops by him an he goes over to it. Probly some tourist askin directions or somethin. Can't see the people in it like, they're too far away but it's probably a pair of bids; typical car for an ahl couple, a green Morris Minor. Must've come for a jaunt to the seaside, sit in their sweet ahl car an eat chips an ice cream as thee watch the sea. Ah. Bless. Maybe this is where thee came on their honeymoon an they're revisiting it, the town an the memories. Rememberin how once thee were young an happy an hopeful. Or maybe one a them's got terminal cancer an wants to see the place where thee honeymooned while thee still can, before thee cark it like, or maybe one of their children got drowned in the sea here and –

Aw, catch yerself on, yeh morbid get, an get yerself home. Gerrout of all this, Stutterin Phil an his drug hunt an the warplane screamin over the memorial with its long long lists of the long dead this whole place is one of mass murder get yerself home to yer rabbit an yer tea an yer bath an yer telly an close the curtains on all this shite an be happy an safe an warm.

Alright.

I double back on meself an leave the castle by the harbour. I'll pass through that an on to Trefechan Bridge. Quickest way home that is, I may beat the rain yet.

Step 10: We continued to take personal inventory and when we were wrong admitted it. Which meant that every second was recorded because every second we breathed and ar hearts went on pumping blood so we continued to feed this sin-stinking raddled upright carcass, all purity and innocence long since defiled, all chalices of wonder long since filled with shit. All living moments not one excepted reeking with ar sickness and ar guilt and ar immeasurable regret an sorrow for being merely us, for being simply born. All the trash in the gas we exhale the gaudy garbage from ar pores ar souls reduced to the skidmarks in ar unwashed kex an this in its entirety broken and awful we jotted down at trembling breakfasts in ar little notebooks, just a little notebook for my inventory, sixty-four pages narrow-ruled, left-hand margin, 159 x 102mm, seventy-nine pence from the Spar.

CAR

Rush hour in this small town and they join the farting crocodile of traffic inching its way round the start of the one-way system. Crawling past B-Wise and beyond that Argos and Iceland and Lidl and past the old train-station buildings now a Wetherspoon's pub. At the roundabout by the twenty-four-hour garage this line of traffic splits into spokes and each one speeds up and Darren puts his foot down.

—Where to, Ally? Where djer reckon?

Alastair shrugs. —Dunno. Just follow the one-wayer, I suppose. See where it takes us, like.

—Yeh keepin yer eyes open, yeh?

—Course, yeh. A one-armed feller I'm lookin for.

—That'll be ar man. Shout if yis see im.

—Will do.

Plenty of people all with four limbs. Dark sheet of sky over all this, this quick movement in this small town and a huge green hump above it all, the monument atop and the glassy hill itself circled by specks of birds. Spilling light from pub and café windows and shapes behind the condensed and cloudy glass of those windows and the pavements busy with people, all with four limbs which Alastair begins to count one arm two arm one arm two arm but then gives up and begins to look for a listing, a mismatched unbalanced cast to all the busy people carrying shopping or pushing prams or just standing at corners or bus stops or leaning against walls.

—Any sign?

—Nah. Thee've all got two arms, Da.

—Keep lookin, well.

Up a narrow sloping street ending in another cross-roads around a town clock built out of bland beige blocks and the high yellow face of the dial. Some benches below that face all occupied by a quartet of jakeys, one dressed head to toe in camouflage gear and one in a filthy orange jacket, this one evidently a Tourette's, yelling gibberish as he is at the passing cars and the clock and at his own knees. Darren dismisses these four faces raspberry red in a small sneer and follows the road signs directly over the crossroads into another narrow bottlenecked road and waits impatient in the queue until he can move down this road and would go further were it not for the unexpected buffer of the sea, all big and blue-black.

—Aw shite. We're on the friggin prom.

Both of them look right then left, right along the curving sweep of the promenade, the hotel façades and frontages of halls of residence and Chinese take-aways and another huge hill at the end of it, this one with a funicular railway spine, and left at the large Old College the stone of its making the colour of bread pitted by spindrift and wind-borne salt. Ahead of them is the pier; pub and curry house and video outlet and flashing, bleeping arcade.

—Which way, lar?

They are blocking the road at the turning and a car honks behind them.

—Fuckin Mister Impatient there. Darren turns in his seat. —ALRIGHT, CUNT! KEEP YER FUCKIN WIG ON, WILL YER! Jesus fuckin Christ . . .

Alastair sees the veins rise. Alastair can feel Darren's frustration and rapidly mounting anger pulling at the skin of his face, making it taut and hot. Alastair says:
—Eeyar, go left.

—What for?

—Well, why not? Head towards the castle, like. Makes as much sense as goin thee other way, dunnit?

Darren turns left without indicating. They pass an old lady on a bench feeding a frantic cluster of gulls and pigeons and then pass the castle, some giant stone skeleton stark and serrated against the navy sky that sky visible through the holes in the ramparts where stones have crumbled and fallen away or where windows or bars once were fitted or nothing at all just a designated hole open to the sky and the weather and the cruciform arrow slits in the east-facing wall just that one wall remaining upright of the east transept like some old film set illusive, unreal. Depthless mirage they circle and skirt and leave behind.

—Now where?

Alastair consults the map on his knee. —Go left again.

—*Left* again?

—Yeh.

—Yer sure about this, Alastair?

—Aye, yeh. It'll take us back into the town, see.

Left again through a warren of terraces all uphill. Old town, some of the stone in the walls of these streets the original stone hewn from the hill on which it was built and used once to form the outhouses and buttresses of the castle which after yet another directed left-turn they find themselves at once more. Darren hisses and drives on to the prom again and pulls up at the kerb, the engine idling.

—Alastair, yeh see that big ahl building there, all in ruins? Well, that's a castle. Now, unless this town has got *two* of the fuckers, which I very much fuckin well doubt, we've just gone in a great big circle. Which means only one thing.

—What?

—That yerra big thick dozy cunt. Giz that fuckin map.

He snatches the road atlas away from Alastair and holds it up to his face. Alastair looks out at the black ruins and at the dark and unruly sea, waves attacking the shingle and if they resemble white horses in any way at all then it is a mustang herd each unbroken and feral rearing then plunging to pound the land as they might a foal-threatening coyote. Or it is kelpies quickly rising teeth-gnashing from slimy blackness leering with soul hunger agog to drag and drown these strangers strayed too far from home.

—Can't make head nor fuckin tail of this. Useless cunt of a thing. Darren chucks the road map over his shoulder on to the back seat to join the mobile phone there and the empty wrappers and flicked snotters.

—The fuck do we –

A jet screams overhead, a vast chainsaw shredding the sky, the screech of its passage an assault on the head. They crane their necks to watch it pass, bank over the vertical coastline and diminish, the noise of its engines fading to a croaking pulse like static in the air.

—Fuck me, that was low.

Darren smiles. —*That's* what we need, in that right? Carpet-bomb the whole fuckin town, like. Napalm the bleedin place. Soon get the one-armed bastard *then*, wouldn't we?

—What're we gunner do, tho, Da? How we gunner find im?

—Dunno. Just keep on lookin, I suppose. Eeyar, let's ask that skinny cunt over there.

Darren points at a thin figure scampering out of the castle grounds and leans over Alastair, a bony elbow in his thigh muscle to wind the window down on that side.

—Ey, lad! EY, LAD!

The thin figure looks up. Glasses and a sparse goatee beard like a malignant growth.

—C'mere, will yeh!

This vision of ill thinness from out of the fallen fortress. Thin physique, thin beard, thin skin draped in leather jacket and jeans and trainers all skimmed thin through years of wearing. And a jerkiness about him, a twitching unsteadiness as he approaches the car warily and leans low to the window. Alastair can see himself distorted in a lens.

—Ey, yeh don't know of any one-armed people who live round here, do yeh? Missin the left arm, like?

—Buh Buh Buh Bill? He's duh duh duh duh duh *dead*.

Darren rolls his eyes, whether at the news or the stammer Alastair can't tell. Alastair's thigh is beginning to hurt from the pressure of Darren's digging elbow.

—Duh duh duh duh died a-a-a-a-a-a-a-*ages* ago.

—Any others?

—Yeh, thuh thuh thuh thuh there *is* one. Juh juh just sss. Sss. Ssssssssss*aw* im in the cuh cuh cuh cuh castle juh just nnnnow.

—Where'd he go?

The man points over his shoulder towards the harbour and the bridge that spans it.

—Th th th th th th *that* way. If yuh yuh hurry yuh yuh yuh m-m-m-m-m-m-might juh juh —

—Learn to talk proper, yeh fuckin biff.

Darren pulls away from the kerb as fast as possible in the old car. Alastair rubs his thigh and watches in the wing mirror the thin figure standing in the road and staring after them.

—Friggin voice on him, lar, Darren says. —Must take the cunt all night to order his first friggin pint. Bastard minged as well, didn't he? Did yeh get the fuckin stink comin off him?

With engine whining they skirt the mast-crammed harbour and pass a pub out of which light and an Elvis song pound. A small blonde woman unpacking shopping from a car boot outside a tall yellow terraced house leaps backwards out of their path and Alastair sees her lofted V-sign silhouette in the rear-view mirror.

—Djer think this is him? Djer think we've got the thievin get?

—Probly, yeh. Can't be many mushers with one arm in a small town like this, can there? This is ar fuckin man, lar. Bet yeh.

The worn brakes squeal as they jerk to a stop at another crossroads and a bus passes in front of them, those shapeless smudged faces behind the mucky glass in the weak yellow light of the interior some mobile aquarium for gilled people, and through its exhaust Darren turns right on to the Trefechan Bridge. The dying evening light and both of them squinting through it at the figures crossing the bridge, a couple holding hands and an old man walking a Labrador and a young man in a thick blue shirt reading a folded paper as he walks and another figure ahead in a dark tartan fleece an bulging carrier bag of shopping in his right hand and a left arm the sleeve of which appears to be hanging loose perhaps empty.

—Fuck me, Alastair, there he fuckin is! We've fuckin found the cunt!

Darren would accelerate but there is a crawling Citroën in front of him. Some granny driving.

—Get out the way, yeh ahl fuckin bag! Give me the hammer, Ally! GIVE ME THE FUCKIN HAMMER, ALASTAIR!

—What fuckin hammer? I didn't know we –

—GET THE FUCKIN HAMMER, YEH FUCKIN –

With his left arm Darren yanks the glovebox open and scrabbles through the shite in there, the empty wrappers and documents and general mess, then scoops it all out over Alastair's knees and on to the floor and there is no hammer, so steering one-handed and the car lurching he leans and gropes underneath his seat and yells a loud non-word vicious and triumphant as he pulls out a lump hammer. Alastair stares at that tool.

—What're yeh gunner do?

—Do? We're gunner do his other fuckin arm, lar! Both fuckin legs n all! Six-pack the fuckin blert is what we're gunner do! PARAFUCKINPLEGIC THE THIEVIN CUNT AN GERROUT THE FUCKIN WAY, WILL YEH, YER AHL FUCKIN BITCH!

Darren spurts speed and bumps the Citroën. Alastair notices a Red Kite Preservation Society sticker on that car's back window as it bursts scared forwards and turns immediately left and Darren hisses a *yessss* and stamps his foot and they pounce towards the man, the engine now beginning to scream. There is another man running towards their target, this man in a donkey jacket with yellow reflective shoulder pads and grinning with his hands behind his back and the hammer's head protrudes from Darren's fist and is bigger than that fist and dense-steel made and there are candles burning in Darren's eyes and a grinding from his mouth as his teeth lock and clench and they are twenty yards away, fifteen, ten.

BRIDGE

Always so windy on this friggin bridge. It can be a bright sunny day, like, not a lick of a breeze then yeh step on to this bridge an that's it, fuckin Typhoon City. Always freezin cold n all, off the sea like, but nice to look over an see the swans an the ducks an the geese an stuff an once last year I saw a seal under there, big fuckin seal swimmin under the boats, amazin magical thing, but right now I'm cold an hungry an I don't wanner look over the bridge at the water I just wanner get home. Me right shoulder's aching from the shoppin bag an me stump's burnin with the cold salt wind an it's a bit fuckin strong, this wind, batterin me head like a blunt instrument or somethin an I just wanner gerrout of it, get home an feed Charlie an feed meself get home safe n warm but, ah shite, here's Perry runnin towards me in that yellow-flash donkey jacket he wears at the tip. Could do without this, really. He'll keep me gabbin for ages, Perry will, an I just wanner friggin be home.

I think about duckin down a side road or somethin an crackin on that I haven't seen him but he's close enough now for me to see his happy face, big grin on his kite, like, an I feel a sudden surge of warmth for him. He looks so happy. I remember as well that he blames himself for his mother freezing to death a year or two ago; he went out on the piss one winter an left her without fuel in her cottage up in the hills an she froze an Perry found her an that was what tipped him over the edge into full-blown alcoholism, like, an since then he has this deep reparative urge to help people, like, an now he's got his arms behind his back, probly concealin some prezzie for me, like, so I stop an wait for him an force meself to smile.

—Iya, Perry.

—Close yewer eyes, then! Got a surprise for yew I yav!

—What is it?

—Member that surprise I told yew about this mornin? Close yewer eyes, now!

He's stood in front of me all grinning, cheeks red with exertion. Breath puffin from him in clouds. He looks *so* happy. I hear a car's engine screaming quite a ways behind me, probly just turnin on to the bridge like, someone raggin it, desperate to get home. Just like fuckin *I* am.

—Perry, I'm knackered, mate, I just wanner –

—No, it's serious! It's good, honest!

This helps him. This bestowing of presents, like, it *helps* Peredur. Keeps him sober, keeps him alive. I put me shoppin bag down an close me eyes. Sigh. Hear him chuckle. Feel me left sleeve bein tugged down an then somethin slidin up that sleeve, somethin smooth an cool nudgin softly against me stump.

Christ, that car's friggin *screamin*. Sounds like thee engine's about to explode. Must be in some fuckin hurry.

—Yur yew go, boy. How's that, then?

I open me eyes an Perry's slid a prosthetic arm up me sleeve an is holding on to the hand of it. We're standin here like that, as if shakin hands. Or, no, *holding* hands. It looks friggin daft an I can't help laughin.

Screamin engine louder.

—See? Told yew I adder present, didn't I? Like it?

I go to say something, fuck knows what, but that engine screamin now right fuckin behind me suddenly stops as the car slams the brakes on right by us at the kerb, just a few feet away. It looks like the same car that called FuhFuhPhil over, thee ahl Moggy Minor. Must still be lost. Two figures inside it, one wearin a baseball cap, stare at me an Perry for a moment, neither face pleased or happy, in fact they look a right fuckin sparky pair an they regard me an Perry for a moment then chug away, over the bridge an into Trefechan. Must be lookin for someone in particular or somethin. Looked fuckin pissed off about somethin. He wants to watch that engine, tho; old car like that, keep tearin thee arse out of it an it'll fuckin fall apart on him.

—What yew reckon, then?

I look down at ar still joined hands, his flesh an mine plastic. —Where djer gerrit from?

—Member I told yew this mornin about-a hospital waste?

—Ah. I take hold of the prosthesis in me right hand an pull it out of me empty sleeve.

—Buffed it up for yew an everythin, I did. Got it lookin all smart, like.

—Ta very much an that, Perry, but I've got one, mate. Ozzy gave me one when thee did the amputation, like. Got fed up wearin it, prefer it without, to be honest. Stuck it in the bottom of me cupboard. Only ever worn it the once.

Standin here like this, one sleeve danglin empty an holdin a false arm in me right one, me *whole* one. Feel like I'm gunner fall over. Feel so unbalanced. Feel like a right twat.

—Yeh, but yew might like *that* one better, tho. Could yew not just give it a go?

His face lookin all sad. Cars passin, passengers starin at us, this peculiar arrangement of limbs. I tuck the falsie into me left armpit, bend an pick up the bag of shoppin.

—Alright well, yeh, I'll give it a go. I'm dead grateful, Perry, honest, it's a fuckin top prezzie. Just not really into prosthetics, tho. Sooner go without.

He sniffs. Then smiles. —Ah well. Thought that counts, mun, innit?

—It is, mate, yeh.

And then the typical abrupt change of mood in Perry, sad to happy in an eyeblink. A legacy of his addictions, his emotions all over the fuckin place. He can cope with that now, tho – that's the difference. That's thee improvement, like.

—Think it's made of wood, he says. —Chuck it on a fire if yew run out-a logs, mun.

That makes me laugh. —Where yis off to now?

—Shop for baccy. An bread an eggs.

—Egg banjo for tea again, yeh?

—Aye, as per usual. Bit-a brown sauce on it. Give yew a knock later, yeh? Get the cards out, is it?

—Yeh, that'd be good. Bout eightish.

—I'll get some HobNobs as well then. Eight o'clock.

—Sound. An ta for thee arm.

He grins an pats me on the shoulder an we go ar separate ways. Another fuckin burden to cart home but at least it's not far now, only a few more minutes. The street lamps buzz an flicker on above me as I head towards Pen-yr-Angor an I see a starling on the bridge balustrade, just standin there with his wings tucked an lookin at me with his head cocked as if he's been watchin me for quite some time. Ah. That's nice. Probly wonderin why I don't look like other humans, why one of me arms is detachable. I click me tongue softly at him an he chirps an flits away, bankin into the wind. Probly headin down towards the pier under which all the other starlings roost. Yeh can see them around this time, dusk like, zippin over the town in clouds. The fuckin *noise* thee make, under the pier, like; a cacophony. It's ace to stand under there amid all the bird racket. So loud. Need a brolly, tho, or yer'll get covered in cack.

Loud an bold, some might say aggressive, bird which walks with a waddling swagger. Successful, common species, gregarious, forming huge flocks outside breeding season especially at favoured roosts. Gloss-black upperparts with marginal brown on wing feathers. Underparts in summer gloss black too but speckled white in winter an red legs yellow bill season-ally unaltering. Short tail an pointed wings make flight silhouette easily recognisable the

starling. The

star . . . ling.

Watchin me like that. Funny little fucker. Wonder what was goin through his daft feathered head.

Final burst of speed now; get the shopping an this ridiculous false arm and yourself home before the rain starts to fall an the cold comes down. Be by the fire eatin yer tea when the rain starts to fall an the cold comes down. Final burst of speed.

Step 11: We sought through prayer an meditation to improve our conscious contact with God as we understood Him, praying only for knowledge of His will for us, and the power to carry that out. As if that knowledge an even the striving for realisation of it wasn't the most shatteringly destructive thing dreamed up by the human mind. As if we wanted ar condition to stand up in front of us in all its stinking sickness pus-filled leering as if that could assist in any way whatsoever as if one single step towards it would result in anything other than a fall through black fathoms without end. We strove an struggled for ar suffering to be rewarded with understanding an through the scoured cells an torn-apart hearts an scorched eyes an melted heads to some of us it came an to me it came as a life underground among wormy earth an bones broke for the marrow an forays into a world above too light too bright an thee only plan for humanity was avoidance on these raids and indeed for ever as all harm seethes in those upright shapes. That was my God, my Higher Power, a life magnified to blinding focus distinct from me and as isolated as the moon, to disguise an despise was its reaction to my reach, to flinch an flee from my gesture. So THAT was helpful, wasn't it?

CAR

—Son of a fuckin *cunt*. Coulda fuckin *sworn* that was im. Did yeh see them, Ally? Pairer fuckin puffs holdin hands in public. Coulda been kids around or anythin. Deserved a wellyin just for doin *that*, the friggin pairer them. Coupla fuckin homs.

—Yeh. Chutney ferrets.

—Shit stabbers.

—Unless thee were just *shakin* hands, Da. Coulda just been *shakin* hands, couldn't thee?

—Nah. Two fuckin quegs them, lar; I could tell. An both of em with *two* fuckin arms n all. That stutterin bastard musta been off his friggin head. Unless he was takin the piss, like . . .

They take the road up and around in a long curve, the street lights flickering on ahead of them as if racing or chasing that electric pulse. Darren flicks the headlights on and the beams splash wonky on the road ahead, one lamp twisted. This squinting car.

—Aw, would yeh look at that. Gozzy fuckin beams n all. Havin a laugh, that twat Tommy, tellin yeh. Gives us a stupid fuckin shitty job an a stupid fuckin shitty ahl shed of a car to do it in. Piss-takin knob'ed, he's gettin a fuckin gobful when we get back to town, tell yeh fuckin *that* fer nowt.

Alastair says nothing, just regards the bottom of the

wide valley below them and the housing estate they drive through spilling down into that valley to join the town proper, the spread orange pepper of its lights in the sudden dusk, the winter evening come quick and early as it must and does. The illuminated brick barns and warehouses of the retail park at the outskirts and then further still the huts and cabins and hangars of the industrial estate, the skinny chimneys and rotund cooling towers steaming. And flanking the whole habitation the opposite high side of the valley, the big dark humps of the carved land elbowed by the ice that once sought the sea now spread at town's edge like the vast lapping tongue of the town or its drool.

A boy in the garden of a council house is tossing a football into the air and catching it again. Throwing it up in the air and catching it again. Alastair watches him as they pass then turns to Darren.

—Ey, Da, I've just had a thought.

—Ah shit. That's *all* I fuckin need.

—No, listen. This one-armed feller; he's probly wearin a falsie, inny? One a them false limbs, like. Here's us lookin for a musher with only one arm but it probly looks like he's got two, knowmean? So we'll *never* fuckin find im, will we?

Yellow-green in the dash light, Darren's face grinds on his neck to look at Alastair. Eyes wide for a moment then they lid and hood.

—What's up?

—You fucking *twat*, Alastair.

This hissed through clenched teeth.

—Why? Wharrav a fuckin done?

—You fucking *twat*. Why didn't yeh fuckin think of

that before? Before I drove us all the fuckin way out here? You stupid fuckin –

—Me? Why didn't *you* think of it?

—Why didn't *I* think of it? I'll tell yeh why *I* didn't fuckin think of it.

Darren pulls over to the kerb by a row of shops, a chipper and a Spar and a post office now shut. The light from the takeaway falls into the car and Darren's looming face is half yellow half shaded and close enough for Alastair to see the blackheads on his nose and feel the warm spit on his face.

—Because *I* was the one doin the fuckin drivin, that's why! Cos *you* acted the CUNT an lost yer fuckin licence!

Alastair's head begins to thump. The back of his tongue dries up in an instant. He cringes back against the door as if trying to physically force himself through it.

—All's *you've* done all fuckin day is fill yer ugly fuckin face with fudge! Who's been doin all the fuckin work, ey? FUCKIN SOFTSHITE HERE, THAT'S OO!

Darren thrashes at his own chest with a rigid forefinger and Alastair hears the hollow thudding. There are long stained teeth very close to his eyes. Teeth that once tore the eyebrow off a screaming face, Alastair saw it, recalls now the mask of blood.

—I didn't have the fucking TIME, did I? Had fuckin things to DO, didn't I, yeh useless fuckin –

—Yeh, but bl bl blame –

—BLEH BLEH BLEH BLEH BLEH!

—Blame Tommy, tho, mate, he –

—Blame Tommy? I'M BLAMIN FUCKIN *YOU*, CUNT!

A big bunched fist hovers. Alastair cringes still further from the fat knuckles and the eyes and the teeth and the stale breath that comes at him in heavy urgent hisses but then all of these things are in a blink away from him, he blinks once and Darren is back in his seat, his elbows on the steering wheel, his face in his hands. Alastair's voice is tiny.

—Sorry, Da, I –

—Shurrup. Just shut the fuck up. Don't say another fuckin word, you fuckin prick.

Alastair doesn't. Simply watches silently as Darren rubs his hands across his face rasprasp and grinds his teeth together. Mutters something inaudible and then says slowly: —Gerrout.

—Get out of the car?

—Gerrout the fuckin car. There's a shop there. You go in there an buy me summin to fuckin calm me down. *You* fuckin wound me up, *you* can fuckin bring me down. Go on, gerrout, knob'ed. Fuck off.

—What kind of –

In one lunge Darren has opened the door on Alastair's side and shoved him out and slammed the door shut again. In his left eye's side he can see Alastair rise up past the window and stand there for a second or two then move away rubbing his elbow into the Spar, the shellsuited skinnyness of him as if taken by that bright portal.

Then Darren sees nothing but the street-light sheen on the dashboard laminate. Focuses on one small specific spot of that, the matt orange reflection which sharpens in his eye as he stares and becomes brighter. Becomes dazzling, some small sun or searchlight that he spits words into.

—This stupid fuckin job. This stupid fuckin car. Fuckwit fuckin Alastair. Tommy fuckin Maguire. Some cunt pays for this shit.

Almost humming, that bright reflected spot. Almost crackling like a desert sun frying Darren's grunted muttered words.

—Tellin yis, some cunt fuckin pays. Better than this fuckin shit, me, don't need this fuckin shit. Fuckwit fuckin Alastair, shitey fuckin car. Fat cunt Tommy Maguire. Shit you not, lar, some fuckin cunt is gunner fuckin gerrit. Fuckin soon *as*. The way it fuckin works, man. Some cunt's gorrer pay. Someone's gorrer get bumped, lar. Pure fuckin *is* gunner happen. *Is* gunner fuckin –

A small crawling darkness through the bright spot. Darren focuses on that, sees wings, recognises a familiar shape: bluebottle on steroids.

—Well, *hello* there, you, yis little fuckin bastard. Fancy seein *you* again.

Sluggish cleg fly with bloodlunch and Darren can pinch its wings and lift it wriggling to his face. The writhing legs and the compound eyes and the grey-striped body. Ungrinning, Darren pinches tighter to see the legs struggle more frantic then simply holds the fly to the dash and presses. Feels a small popping against his fingertips, small warm splash of his own blood returned, robbed and now reclaimed. Smears the mess off the dash with his thumb then wipes that thumb across Alastair's seat and feels the heat from his arse.

—*Some* cunt's gunner pay, tho. Fuckin *deff*o. Fuckin soon *as*.

Alastair gets back in, a bulging Spar bag on his lap. Darren pulls away from the kerb, U-turns and heads back into town.

—See if we can see that stutterin prick. Quick look an then we'll fuck off home. Whatjer get me?

Alastair opens the bag and peers into it. —Bag of crisps.

—What kind?

—Monster Munch.

—What flavour?

—Spicy.

A nod. —What else?

—A pasty. Packet of Jaffa Cakes. A butty, I think it's ham. A Scotch egg an a can of Lilt an a Mars bar.

—Giz thee egg an the can. An open em for me, will yeh? I'm drivin.

Alastair does. Back into the town and back on to the Trefechan Bridge. Darren mumbles through a gobful of food, spraying breadcrumbs like saliva turned to sand.

—An keep yer fuckin eyes peeled.

Alastair does that too.

—Or I'll peel em fuckin for yeh.

—Alright.

HOME

Tell yeh what, tho, I mean, I've got to admit it – it's absolute *shite*, only havin one arm. You miss it sometimes, with real pain; like when there's shoppin to carry, or when you're in the shower, or yeh smile at a pretty girl an she smiles back then looks down at yer torso an the smile goes or turns into a kind of grimace. Pity or disgust, each one's unbearable. Or like when yer on the beach at night-time an the wind's pickin up into a storm and yeh stand in it an yeh wanner feel part of it an you hold yer arms out, wantin to embrace it like, so yeh do that as best yeh can an there yeh are all fuckin lopsided, unbalanced like, one side of you all truncated an stubby an daft. Or like when yer arms involuntarily shoot up, like when yeh wanner get someone's attention or when, say, Stevie Gerrard sprints up from midfield an batters the net with a screamin thirty yarder an yer arms shoot up automatically, watchin the game on Sky with the Group or in Perry's shack with the dish he scavved off the tip an yer arms go up an yer up off yer seat an there you are, standin there again all friggin lopsided. Lookin stupid. It can be shite, only havin one arm. It can be awkward an humiliating an you feel horribly ill-equipped for living in the world. I wish I still had two. I really fuckin do.

More street lights flickerin on as I walk down

Pen-yr-Angor, wind off the sea bringin ocean smells an the crying of the gulls. Rain's held off all day but it's gunner chuck it down soon, I can sense it. Smell it, even. Still see the big black clouds in the sky gone grey now, dark grey with a couple of stars glittering, them clouds gettin fatter an heavier, all bulging, just at the point of bursting. Me shoulder's *really* friggin complainin now, with the weight of the shoppin like, an so's me left half-arm with the pressure of squeezin the prosthetic in me armpit but I grit me teeth an ignore it all an pass the sailin club an the pathway up to Pen Dinas where the one-eyed fox lives an the World War II pillbox an then I'm at me door, that's it, thank fuckin God, at last I'm home.

I put the shoppin down, feel me shoulder muscles relax. Get me key out, open the door, hang me key on the hook, pick up me shoppin, close the door with me bum. Inside me home now I am. All dry an safe.

But not warm, tho. It's fuckin freezin. I go into the livin room, put the shoppin on the couch, lift me stump so that the falsie thumps to the floor, turn on some lights an the telly an close the curtains then turn on the gas fire. Crouch down to rub me hands together in front of the sputterin flames an then remember that that's somethin I can't do. Can't even do that. See what I mean? It's *shite* only havin one arm.

Shoppin into the kitchen, hoisted up on to the worktop. Dig in it for the celery an snap a stick off with me teeth an switch thee outside light on an go outside into the garden.

—Charlie . . . oh Charlie boy . . . comen get yer celery . . .

Somethin's wrong. Somethin's gone badly fuckin wrong. The hutch door is open an swingin, creakin in the wind. There is the musky whiff of fox an also another smell behind it, both shitty an meaty an there is an unmoving hump of somethin at thee edge of me cabbage run that wasn't there this morning. *Two* humps, actually.

—Oh fuck.

So strong, that fox stink. Can almost friggin *taste* it, like. Must've caused this carnage only a few minutes ago, to leave his niff still lingerin like this. Squirting his musk everywhere, lettin everythin know that this was created by him, signing this mess an murder with his squirted scent.

You left the fuckin hutch door unlocked, didn't yeh? Dickhead, yeh forgot to lock the hutch door when yer left the house this morning. This is your fault.

Havin only one arm is absolute *shite*.

I close an lock the hutch door pointlessly then go over to me cabbage run. Two humps; one is Charlie's head, without face or ears. Thee other is Charlie's body, all four feet an tail intact but the body itself just an empty, deflated furry bag as if all thee insides have been slurped out. Not much spilled blood at all. A bad smell. A stillness.

I'm still holdin the celery. Holdin the stick of celery in me one hand like a pathetic weapon. I chuck it over the hedge then fetch me trowel from the lean-to an walk out into the middle of me vegetable patch, the square of bare earth there where I bury compost an intend to grow strawberries next summer an I crouch an dig one-handedly a hole. Into the moist soil an decaying compost, all my leavings, the worms wriggling an the black beetles scurrying an the wind whistlin in me ears an one green foxy eye is watchin all this from the hedge or the hill beyond. I can feel that eye on me. You're always bein watched by *some-thing*. There's *always* some kind of eye on you. Then I go back an pick up the featureless head with the trowel an drop it in the hole then do the same thing with the drained body an everything there is is here at me feet, a wrecked life in a hole. Robbed of feature. Face and heart stolen an destroyed an what's left dumped in the ground, this is it, it's all there is, all that we yearn for dismantled in terror and in pain and buried. Put upon the dirty world. We're on it and it's in us this filthy fucking earth.

Step 3, God

as we understood Him

back to Step 2

restore us to sanity

marry this to the willing adoption of responsibility and sponsoring. Let something else take charge of you while you take charge of something else.

Then forget to lock the fucking hutch.

I pile the earth back on to what's left of Charlie an pat it down with the trowel. He'll be good compost, he will. For me strawberries, like. Then I dig another hole at thee end of the grave an go back inside me house trekkin mudprints fuckin everywhere an fetch Perry's prosthetic present an take it out into the garden an stick thee elbow end of it into the new hole an pack the muck around it to keep it standing. Looks good – this white false hand reaching from thee earth.

Tombstone for Charlie an somethin for me strawberries to cling to when thee start to grow next year. An from now on whenever I come out here, into me garden, it'll be like thee earth is wavin to me. Or Charlie himself, in that earth. An that'll be nice.

—See ya, Charlie. Sorry I left yer door open, mate.

An imagine it in centuries' time, this stuff bein dug up, the false arm an Charlie's bones. Future archaeologists here with their wee brushes an delicate tools, unearthing all this stuff, wonderin what the fuck it all means, what it could possibly signify. All import lost, gone, impossible to reclaim. Just some bones in thee earth an a model of a human arm. Maybe rabbits'll be extinct by then. Maybe this'll be a find of great significance, written up in scientific journals an made the subject for lectures. On telly an everythin. Or vidscreens or watch-o-trons or whatever the fuck we'll call TVs by then. That'll be good, Charlie, won't it? Mess up some future minds, like.

Aw, me little rabbit mate. I'm so sorry. I'm a fuck-up. Kicked the booze an got away and found some sort and degree of happiness but I'm still a fuck-up, I'll *always* be a fuck-up. I'll never be anything but a failure and a smear and I'm so, so sorry.

For everything.

For every flying jumping swimming crawling walking . . .

While I'm out here, I dig up a cabbage an some carrots an a few spuds for me tea. It needs weeding, this vedge patch; nettles an dandelions an all sorts growin across the drills. I'll do it tomorrow. Rip up all the competitors, these plants out of place. Maybe

leave a few dandelions, cos I'll piss the bed if I pull
em up. Plus I like the splash of colour they add, that
yellow, like. That bright yellow

turnin grey to black an eventually mush that sweet
sickly smell

flowers like me arm

dead flowers like my fucking arm

I leave the trowel in thee earth an bundle the vedge
up against me chest gettin me fleece all mucky an go
back into the kitchen an dump the vedge in the sink
an turn the radio on an wash the vedge well, gettin
rid of all the

spots of blood thick and purple teeth and rending
trauma trauma

clinging soil an slugs an aphids, tryin to hold the
spuds an carrots against the sink bottom an scrub them
with one hand an it's not easy an sometimes I fuckin
hate all this one-armed shite. Really fuckin *hate* it.
Fuckin Rebecca, I hope you know what you've fuckin
done to me not that I think you'd care. I hope you're
clean, too. I hope you're hating every minute of your
life. I hope you're happy like me. Wherever the fuck
you are I hope you

so sorry

so sorry

Try to peel an chop spuds an carrots an cabbage
with only one fuckin arm. Puttin pies in thee oven is
easy, but try an open the bastard box with one hand.
It's a cunt. It's a

horror horror nightmare stop I hate this life I hate
this world I cannot live I I I I

Lots of vedge on to boil. Half for me, an I'll put

half outside in the garden for the one-eyed fox cos he'll be back in the morning for his breakfast. Probly asleep in his hole now, his burrow like, all aslumber as he digests Charlie. Surrounded by bones crunched for the marrow, sleepin off his successful raid on the strange an dangerous world above.

I'm sorry, Charlie. So sorry.

please

stop this

make it better

As I'm watchin *Changing Rooms* an waiting for me food to cook, I hear a knock at the door, too early for it to be Perry. I go to answer it but there's no one there; probably just the wind, rattlin the letter box, like. It's really picked up now, an the rain's finally come, lashin against the door an the windows like flung gravel. So just the weather calling, the rain an the wind come knocking, an it'll be Perry, motherless Perry, in about an hour or so, but sooner or later there's gunner be a rap on the door that I won't be expecting. It'll come. Don't want it to, like, it's not something I want to happen, but I *know* it fuckin will.

I *know* it.

Step 12: Having had a spiritual awakening as a result of these steps, we tried to carry this message to addicts, and to practise these principles in all our affairs. And the sheer scale of this imperative struck us utterly dumb. We walked blinking into the sunlight and whatever feeble release awaited us, still-smoking lobes devastated and scorched, and what was expected of us dizzy children, us spent matches, was heavy enough was hot enough was so truly horrible enough that some of us scurried as far away from it as we possibly could, back into the shadows reseeking the cool earth. Any moisture to plunge into to soothe ar sizzling skin. And all of us entabulated, calibrated and judged by some remote and watching will continually vigilant and alert to transgression and this is how it must be for us, this issue confused and scared, this regimen rigid and bone-stiff must from now on be our apparel because stripped of it will come the ripping, the surrender, the night-time knock at the door. And what's good for us is GOOD for us so whittle yerself into one blunt point an keep it aimed away from you an make no mark, scratch no surface, you've done too much of that for ever. Let the world in. Mere and just. And in this wise it won't shred you.

CAR

The rain has come in a downpour ferocious and battering and it feels like fists assaulting the car roof, pumpkin fists of a crouching ape pummelling and buckling the metal roof. Two circuits of the small town saturated, no people to be seen, most sheltering, and how to tell through the teeming water of what secrets carried by these bedraggled stragglers, what histories maybe of horror and of loss? What differences portered beneath their sopping surfaces, what hidden nothings? Some targets all without exception but impossible to tell which is theirs.

—Well. Looks like it's fucked, lar.

They have parked up on the promenade once again by the castle and with the engine off the true timbre of the rain can be felt in skull and lung and the gulls can be heard wailing as if hopelessly lost in the wet and outer darkness and no way back whatsoever. Only the groan and click of the wipers clearing the screen of water clear visibility for one half-second and then the glass rerunning. Like this drench has come from buckets thrown at close proximity and not from the remote clouds way up there in the flat and pressing greyness, as if that great distance is no obstacle offered to the need to swamp and drown the trodden-on earth and those that tread and the dizzying depth of that needing.

—Fuckin *pissin* down, man. Fuckin look arrit. Like a friggin monsoon or summin.

—Wharrer we gunner tell Tommy?

Darren shakes his head. —Ah fuck, *I* don't know, do I? Fat cunt'll probly send us back.

—Fuck *that*, man.

—Is right, Alastair. Couldn't find the cunt today, not gunner find im tomorrer, are we? Doan even know what he looks like. Look for a feller with one arm, aye, alright, but what if he's wearin a fuckin false one? How the fucker we supposed to recognise im then? Fuckin Tommy. Tellin yeh; thick as pigshit, that bastard. Honest to God. Head like a sack of shite. Worse than *you*, lar, I shit you not. Muchos fuckin dumb.

Alastair says nothing, just stares out the window at the castle ruins black behind the opaque grey curtain of rain. Darren digs the ham sandwiches out of the Spar bag between his feet and rips the packet open and takes out one butty and plonks it down on Alastair's knee.

—Eeyar, you.

—Ta.

—Not that yeh fuckin deserve it like or anythin.

And they sit in silence eating, just the wipers' sweep and the calling gulls and the relentless drum of the rain. And somewhere behind all that the crash and hiss of the sea on the shingle and the slow surge of the retreating water felt rather than heard as a tingle at the base of the spine or a tweak at the amphibian brain.

—Fuckin *hate* this, I do, Darren says.

—What, the ham butty?

—No, not the fuckin ham butty, softlad. I'm talkin about when a job goes tits up. When, yer know like, yeh can't get the fuckin thing sorted. Like that time we chased that Scottish cunt all the way out to Speke fuckin airport, remember that one?

Alastair nods chewing.

—Tryna catch the bastard before he reached his fuckin plane back to fuckin Glasgow.

—Didn't friggin gerrim, did we?

—That's what I'm sayin. Frustratin as all fuck, it is. Member the cunt wavin to us from the steps, like? Them stairs up into the plane?

Alastair nods again, remembering the small figure waving and too remembering the ensuing chaos. Darren's frustration venting and the teeth and the repeated kicks in the pub dragging the broken crawling pleading leaking person out from under the pool table so he could be kicked again in soft places once bony.

—Yeh, I fuckin well *hate* this shit, I do. Darren eats the last bite of butty and wipes his hands on his knees and Alastair does the same. —Come ed, well. Might as well fuck off, ey?

Alastair shrugs. —Suppose so, aye.

Darren turns the ignition key. The engine coughs then whines then catches.

—Fuckin car. Fuckin Tommy. Piecer fuckin shite . . .

—Think it'll get us back?

—Fuckin hope so, lar. Don't fancy havin to kip out in *this*, do you?

They drive back through the town wet and empty and climb the slope past the hospital and university back into the hinterland. Almost full night now and the street lights already sparse, the world shrinks to the misshapen splash of illuminated gleaming tarmac immediately beyond the bonnet and the needles of rain slanting through that leaning light. Wet blackness on each side and also above, the heavy cloud cover allowing no moon nor no dim cinders.

—Still got that postie to screw, haven't we?

—What postie?

—That fuckin post office back up north. The one where yeh bought that fudge an helped thee ahl girl out like a fuckin divvy when she dropped yer change. Remember?

—Oh aye, yeh. Alastair nods firm. —Will it still be open, tho?

Darren shrugs. —Still fuckin screw it if it's not, can't we? Don't matter if it's open or not, like, does it? Tellin yeh, the brewstered fuckin locals use it as a bank, too fuckin lazy to drive into Chester or Wrexham or a bigger town, like. Fuckin megabucks, lar. How's that sound?

—Least we'll have summin to show Tommy.

—Yeh, well, let's think about that fat get when we need to, like. He might not need to know anythin about this. Might not need to have fuck all to do with it, knowmean? Just me n you, lar. Pure two-way split. No other cunt needs to know, do thee?

—No.

—You *know* it, Ally. Light us up, will yeh? An old on to yeh fuckin seat cos I'm gunner put me fuckin foot down. Pure cannot *wait* to screw that postie, no fuckin lie.

Darren puts a cigarette in his mouth and Alastair does too then strikes a match. Fluttering orange feather-flame flits from face to face in the dark car interior, the old and chugging rain-dripping car, rattling and banging as the engine is forced into acceleration, the loosening bodywork, the battered dash, the rocked hammer beneath the driver's seat. The ground around them begins to rise again as they leave the sea behind and in one of the million trees they pass just outside Tal-y-Bont and unseen by them an owl, a barn owl, roosting ghost in the top tossed limbs regards their slow wet passing and will at some point in the night ahead plunge and wreck some smaller, weaker life when all signs of their traffic have gone. Destroy and devour this bird will, lit by no light, in no emission from the trundling car which continues to move away from disappointment and towards purpose. Towards purpose, and between two bloods.